"The Imp of Mischief obtrudes the board, and obstructs Ezekiel's vision.— *See pages* 28 *and* 31.

THE MISHAPS

OF

Mr. EZEKIEL PELTER.

ILLUSTRATED.

THIRD EDITION.

CHICAGO:
S. C. GRIGGS AND COMPANY.
1875.

LAKESIDE
PUBLISHING & PRINTING CO.
CHICAGO.

Preface.

The author of this volume proposes, simply, through imaginary persons and a succession of amusing situations, to expose certain social errors; an attempt amply justified by authentic precedents, and the known existence among us of characters and associations like those herein presented.

The Satire—if it is so regarded—will be found, in its ENTIRETY, *to be free from reflection upon any legitimate and consistent organization for charity or good works; and its spirit, if considered from the standpoint of the writer, and as he conceived it, cannot offend the most fastidious admirer of Christianity and good morals.*

The Author.

LIST OF ILLUSTRATIONS.

CONTENTS.

CHAPTER I.

CHAPTER II.

CHAPTER III.

CHAPTER IV.

CHAPTER V.

CHAPTER VI.

CHAPTER VII.

CHAPTER VIII.

CHAPTER IX.

CHAPTER X.

CHAPTER XI.

CHAPTER XII.

CHAPTER XIII.

CHAPTER I.

FLOWERS FROM A MORAL GARDEN, AND THEIR SEPARATE SCENTS.

THERE are men yet living in New York, who will remember, if properly reminded, "Old Israel Smith;" unless his modest etchings "on the sands of time" have been washed away by the shifting currents of our social and commercial life.

Smith is a very common name; but *Israel* Smith is *not* so common.

If Israel could have known to what strange mistakes such a common name as Smith would lead, without some *prænomen* more *un*common, he never would have named his children John and Joseph. But he did so name them, and their strange experiences — or some of them — form the cocoon from which the author weaves the following story.

The boys were twins. So alike were they in personal appearance, that even among familiar friends one was often mistaken for the other. Their likeness was not a *general* resemblance simply, leading to occasional mistakes in their identity;

it was a *perfect* likeness, to the eye of ordinary observation, and to nice perceptions a distinction was found difficult. Even by their parents—when the boys were not together—John was often miscalled "Joe," and Joseph "John."

When they were *together*, it was possible to observe such a difference in *expression*, as to give to each his own identity; but this was not so marked as to be observed when they were apart.

If, to any one, a resemblance so *exact* seems unnatural, or opposed to the common observation of mankind, we prove the doctrine of exceptions by this well-authenticated fact: and the fact is perfectly consistent with proper analogic reasoning. All of us have seen twin-born children bearing *some* resemblance to each other; and *some* of us have seen such a resemblance as confuses a casual observer. If, then, Nature, in well-known cases, so approaches an exact similitude, is it not reasonable to suppose that, in instances exceptional, Nature *may* so fashion twins as to make the resemblance *perfect?*

But, independent of all reasoning, we have the fact; and that, for us, is all-sufficient.

They had their father's features; and his were of that sober order, usually employed by sanctimonious spirits in making what is called "God-fearing men." Why pattern men are called "God-fearing," rather than "God-loving," is only comprehended by lugubrious souls. Israel was a pattern man: that is, he made long prayers, with one eye open to our fleshly wants.

As the boys grew up, they developed dispositions most *un*like; and this, to Israel, was a perpetual "cross."

"If John could only be like Joseph!" was his pious exclamation, always ended by a pious sigh, when the boys were mentioned in his presence.

Joseph was familiar with the history of that Bible character for whom he had been named; and he said — whatever may have been his thought — that if the wife of another Potiphar should try *him* with lascivious charms, he would prove a Joseph in his virtue, as he was in name.

John was the object of solicitude and prayer: he was the "bad boy"— the unregenerate — and his solemn visage was a mask, behind which laughed perennial Fun.

He was much about the wharves, and listened with enthusiasm to graphic pictures of the "perils of the deep," of genial climes where Summer is perpetual, and where Oriental charms grace sensuous pleasures.

Joseph sometimes went with John, and *he* found a fund of entertainment in the strange enchantments of the sea. He listened with attentive ear to stories of untutored savages, in islands far away, and of how they lived in the supreme contentment of their own simplicity. His pious ardor was aroused, and he was all impatience to plant, in such a fruitful soil, the seeds of discord and dogmatic disputation.

"What a field for missionary work!" was Israel's commentary, as Joseph told the stories o'er.

Each of the boys began, unconsciously, to prefigure in his mind the coming years; and, before they were old enough for any *actual* service, they made their mimic voyages in their mother's wash-tub. When they had reached a proper age, Israel found them places, on different vessels; each for a lengthy voyage: Joseph—the pride of Israel's heart—for the South Pacific; and John—the unregenerate—for the glamours of the Orient.

After this, for thirty years, they roved the seas; and during all that time they did not see each other. They made occasional returns to the family home, but, it so happened, their visits were at different times.

About ten years after the boys had shipped as nascent tars, the good man Israel, on a bed of sickness, began to make the final footings in the ledger of his life, that he might find a proper balance to show against the unseen book of the world to come. He must have found the balance favorable, for, with a complacent smile, and without a murmur or regret, he left a benediction in the flitting air, and gave up the ghost.

His wife had gone before him; and, being ever faithful, perhaps she had gone to sweep and garnish, with celestial fingers, in the promised house, as, for many years and with flagging strength, she had swept and garnished in the house of Mundus, against the time of Israel's coming.

With the snapping of these cords of life, the connecting link between John and Joseph Smith was also snapped. Neither knew, with certainty, where the other could be found; and they soon discovered that there were so many other John and Joseph Smiths that the common name was like another sea to them, and they were *merged* in it.

When rain-drops fall, from clouds surcharged, they patter on our shingles with their separate beats; but when they fall upon the sea they give no separate sounds, and only serve to swell the mighty roar which swallows them. For Israel's shingles, these boys each had his separate sound; but when plunged in the *sea* of Smiths, they soon were wholly lost, and not so much as a phosphorescent glimmer marked where they had fallen.

At the date of the following incidents, years had passed since either had received a word of information in relation to the other, and neither knew that the other was alive.

Both of them were saving of their money; and they improved each opportunity to increase the store. In every port where bargains could be had, they made such purchases as they had transportation for; and then they sold or bartered them at other ports, where generous profits could be realized. Such perpetual accretions, through three decades—added to their pay—made at last a sum quite snug; for, with their occasional promotions, their field for barter and their transportation limits were enlarged.

Their natural dispositions remained unchanged in every changing scene; unless there was a change in Joseph, where there seemed to be a growth of pious zeal in the cause of foreign missions.

Some stories have been told of Joseph, reflecting on his honesty when entrusted with merchantable supplies for contented savages, who, in reality, needed no supplies; but as to all of these reports there was the proverbial "other side," which, in Joseph's view, cleared the ugly shades away, and left his record like a sunny sky, after scudding clouds have passed, looking brighter for their passage.

What was he to do with a useless cargo? Clothing, for example, suited to the climate of the Northern Pole, was hardly suitable for the natives of the South Pacific. Spasmodic charity did not stop to think of this; and why should not Joseph make some fitter disposition? If he was offered money for the cargo, should he refuse to take it? Was it not a providential "lift" for him, and to no one's injury? Surely the natives, to whom it had been sent, had no use for it.

Joseph could reason on these doubtful questions most adroitly; and I can not do him justice in the statement of his nice distinctions.

> "He could distinguish, and divide
> A hair, 'twixt south and southwest side."

John, with his blunt perceptions in matters ethic, might and would, undoubtedly, have called the whole transaction by an ugly name. But John could never comprehend such questions.

Both at length returned to their native city; each with a resolve to quit the sea, and find the comforts of a settled home.

They found the city now much changed from what it was when Israel first began to tell them of its wickedness, and for a time they felt like strangers.

The remarkable resemblance of their childhood was still preserved, and similar employments had given them a similar physical development; even in complexion they were the same, being bronzed by like exposures.

Within a year after their return, both were married.

Their wives were as different, in each distinctive physical development, as can be well imagined; and in mind and temperament they were as far apart.

John's wife was Julia. Perpetual sunshine rested on her face, and beamed in all her smiles. Her heart was a perennial spring, and bubbling fun gave music to its constant flow. She was well developed in every turn of form and limb, and was comely in her look. In activity, she was as supple as an antelope, and could almost rival an athlete. She had looked behind John's somber mask, and found a congenial spirit there; with this she toyed and coquetted for awhile, and then she embraced and loved it. Before their marriage, she gave John due notice of the quickness of her jealous choler; and after marriage, she was not wanting in occasional reminders of it.

John was not at all disturbed by this, for, by nature, he was constant, and Julia was supreme in his affections.

Joseph's wife was Rachel—an incarnate Penetential Sigh. Meekness, and a constant sense of *worminess*, were prominent in her professions.

"All of us are worms!" she frequently remarked, in her sprightly style of conversation.

Her lack of every subtle grace and charm was, to her, a most consoling fact, since it protected her from vanity.

"The besetting weakness of our sex!" as she sententiously observed.

In her angular construction, she formed an outward type of her inward nature; and all her juices were acidulated. Nearly every one believed her to be a hypocrite; but Joseph found in her the chrysalis of an unfledged saint.

With such wives—whose virtues will hereafter more strikingly appear—John and Joseph settled down, but in different sections of the city.

Being differently engaged, even here, they did not chance to run across each other; and having names like scores of others, *these* were insignificant. Each believed the other to be still upon the sea.

Both had the means of living well, and they did live quite respectably.

Soon after this, Joseph's missionary zeal began to find its social trumpeters; and it was not long before "The Ladies' Board of Foreign Missions," then in the flush of its first enthusiasm, became excited by reports of his marvelous adventures.

It was at once determined by the Board that his experience would be, to them, invaluable; and

Mr. Pelter — Ezekiel Pelter — was instructed to secure Joseph's presence.

Mr. Pelter was the oleaginous member of the Board, and he advised the ladies in the business details of their work.

Sanctimonious scents always perfumed his oily chunks of wisdom, and made them most agreeable. He was so in love with charity, that he *lived* on it: not in a shabby, slip-shod way, but quite genteelly. "Charity suffereth long, and is kind," saith the preacher; and Ezekiel Pelter was a living proof of it. If his right hand ever did a stroke of honest labor, it was done so cunningly that his left hand knew not of it.

He called himself, sometimes, a vessel; sometimes a worm; and sometimes the most debased of sinners; but he did not really *think* himself a vessel, or a worm, or a sinner even; and when he addressed his Maker (as he did on every possible occasion) it was in such a patronizing way as to show at once that he thought himself entitled to a special hearing, and that God was honored by his notice.

Except when devotionally engaged, or administering some pious admonition, a perpetual blandness settled on his shining face, and gave impressive unction to his learned speech; and he was never known to differ in opinion from anyone who might extend a favor.

He was addressed, and spoken of, in various ways — and sometimes in *peculiar* ways. Among those most familiar were the following:

By his wife — "PELTER!"

She spoke the name with a sharp and snapping sound, as though her jaws were hung on springs of steel.

He always made quick movements when he heard this voice; for, when unusually excited, she could make the air cerulean; — and she *did*, sometimes.

This was Ezekiel's "cross" — this wife of his — and the ladies of the Board, without exception, pitied him. When he discovered that they pitied him, he bore his cross like a crusader in the Holy Wars — always conspicuous. It is said that he could dissolve the Board in tears by his pictures of domestic trials, and that on such occasions his large and spotless handkerchief played a leading part.

By the badgered — "Pelter, AGAIN!"

These words were spoken usually as profane men utter maledictions; but Ezekiel's mail was proof. When the ladies heard the maledicent tone they were righteously indignant; but when they saw Ezekiel with such a calm and placid look, and such an impressive gesture of his hand, wave the offensive words away, their anger was forgotten in their growing admiration.

"*He* was persecuted," Ezekiel would say; and the effect was magical.

One of the sisters, more emotional than the rest, would even clasp his hand and raise her tearful eyes to his in an actual *over*flow of sympathy.

By the naughty boys—"Old *Pelter!*"

Ezekiel was *too* old a pelter, and too *wise* a one, to attack these wandering Arabs of the street; and as a duck sheds rain from its oily back, he shed the pelts of *gamin.*

By the ladies of the Board—"Mr. *P-e-l-t-e-e-r*," with a lingering, loving accent, which always seemed to touch his noble heart.

Before *this* he bowed, with his hand upon his waistcoat. What emotions were unspoken there, and covered by that hand, they could easily imagine.

Such "Ladies' Boards" are organized, ostensibly, for foreign service; and it is supposed that they employ themselves in the affairs of distant countries. We see them mount their instruments for indefinite ranges, and, with ostentatious bearing, prepare to sweep the distant heavens. Admiring this sublime astronomy, we look for new developments and visit the observatory; the telescope is there, swinging on its axis, in the bisected dome, but it creaks with the rust of long non-usage as it swings. Where are the observers?

" The lingering, loving accent, touched his noble heart."

We find them looking, not through *it*, but through their little microscopes, and chattering like a roost of magpies, as they search for stains upon their neighbors' garments.

To such ignoble ends, come, sometimes, these great pretensions!

The Board, of which Ezekiel was a member, had *its* supply of microscopes; and the ladies were quite expert in the use of them. It was thought—among themselves—that there was not so much as a single "beam" in all their eyes, and that this enabled them to look, with unclouded vision, for "motes" in the eyes of others. What would have seemed to them suspicious, if observed in one *outside* the Board, was regarded with complacency, and even with approval, in a member of the Board.

The emotional member—who would sometimes take Ezekiel's hand, and overflow with sympathy—will serve to illustrate.

Her name was Miranda Trap; or, as Ezekiel loved to call her, "My-*rindy*." By other members, she was spoken of as "peculiar sometimes"; and, by the irreverent, she was oftener spoken of as "gushing."

If *she* was a vessel—and she sometimes claimed to be—she was a genuine Antique, and, beyond a question, cracked; for, upon the slightest provocation she would leak, most copiously.

"Them tears! My-*rindy*," Ezekiel would say, with his hand upon her head; and then he would wrestle with his own emotion. Let future poets call her Niobe.

To borrow here the poetic name, Niobe had found that a "fellow-feeling" makes us *wondrous* kind; and, to such questionable lengths did this feeling bear her ardent soul, that she burned to break Ezekiel's cross, and to anoint him with her tearful unguents.

Ezekiel was not so cold or passionless as not to feel Miranda's sympathy; and it was very precious to him. So this good man found here a refuge from domestic storms.

The ladies of the Board observed occasional displays of tenderness between them; but they never frowned, for they knew Ezekiel's trials and the spiritual nature of his comforter.

Had not the Board determined to send for Joseph Smith, it is difficult to say what might have been the issue of this growing fervor between Ezekiel and Miranda; and perhaps some poisonous flower might have blossomed from it, to infect the moral garden of the Board.

What happened, is reserved for another chapter.

CHAPTER II.

MR. PELTER MAKES A SAD DISCOVERY.

Mr. Pelter knew where Joseph lived; and, in company with others, he had seen him at his house.

When there, Ezekiel, in his peculiar and impressive way, displayed his fascinations; and so successfully, that Joseph was decidedly impressed by them. By many little marks of deference and respect Joseph showed his admiration for Ezekiel, who seemed, in spiritual nature, of kin to him.

If the good man swelled a little as he noticed this, it was but natural; and in this he showed that, in trivial things, he did not exalt himself above humanity, as he did in greater things.

Afterward Ezekiel reported to the Board some of Joseph's conversation, but he could not spice it with the new and strange aromas which Joseph gave to it. What he did repeat only served to tantalize the Board, and to make the members eager to behold this hero of a hundred tales. Miranda Trap, among the others, listened, with wide-eyed wonder, to Ezekiel's report; for, in it, he himself was prominent. She, too, insisted that, if possible, Joseph should be brought to them.

They were so impatient that they resolved to wait beyond their usual time; for, if Mr. Pelter *should* bring the traveler back with him, he might advise them in their work: it was visionary work, though they called it *mission*-ary, and in their view of things it was all the same.

Ezekiel did not know, and in fact he was inclined to question, whether, at such an hour in the day Joseph could be found at home; but he yielded to the ladies' wishes with his usual urbanity, and took his broad-brim hat, and, with a twirl of his large and spotless handkerchief around it, to make it "slick," he bowed and started off.

While jostling through the Broadway throng, with his eyes upon the street, that he might call a stage when the proper one should come, he came in heavy contact with a passer-by. The passer-by was much more earnest than polite in what he said to him, and when Ezekiel turned, with—

"I beg your *par*-don, sir," upon his lips, the passer-by was out of sight.

"*Bless* me!" said Ezekiel.

Whether he was speaking to the passer-by, or

invoking blessings on himself, or addressing one on whom his eyes were fixed, it is impossible to say. He saw a familiar face, with a look of amusement on it, turned in his direction.

Holding out one hand, and with the other lifting off his broad-brim hat, he approached the wearer of the smiling face.

"How *do* you do," said he, impulsively.

"I am very well, sir," was the quiet answer; and the smiling face was merrier than before.

"I was on my way to *see* you, sir," continued Mr. Pelter; and now he made another offer of his hand.

The smiling eyes did not appear to know him, nor did their owner take the offered hand.

"My name is *Pelter! Ezekiel* Pelter! of the *Missionary* Board!" the good man still continued; and now his blandness was like a halo around his smiling face. "Do you not *remember* me?"

"There is some mistake, no doubt," replied the smiling stranger, "for I never saw you, sir, and the name of Pelter was never on my log-book."

"Surely you are Mr. *Smith?*" said Ezekiel, puzzled.

"Oh, yes; and there are a thousand *other* Smiths," replied the stranger, pleasantly.

"But," said Mr. Pelter, with assurance, "you are the son of *Israel* Smith! and have lived for thirty years upon the sea! There are not a thousand 'other Smiths' to answer *this* description!"

"You *do* appear to know me," said the stranger, in surprise; "but, for the life of me, I can't make you out! Perhaps it is your *rig* that 's strange. In what waters did we meet?"

Now Mr. Pelter was not pleased by this reply, for he believed that Joseph Smith had noticed him *particularly*, and it was something new, in his experience, to have *any one* forget him.

Had this been Joseph Smith, he would have been remembered; for Joseph had admired the oily look and words of Mr. Pelter. But this was John, *not* Joseph, Smith.

With a chagrined and injured look, Mr. Pelter now continued:

"The *ladies* would be pleased to meet you at their rooms."

"What ladies?" inquired John.

This question was a fresh offense, for Joseph had expressed a *special* wish to meet the ladies of the Board.

With a crushing dignity and his severest look of pious indignation, Ezekiel now replied: "The Ladies' Board of Foreign *Missions*, sir!"

Unscathed by the lightning of Ezekiel's glance, and all unconscious of his anger, John again inquired:

"And what do they want of *me?*"

This was too much, even for *Christian* equanimity; and Mr. Pelter would have turned away from him with sublime contempt, had he not remembered with what a flourish he had described to the ladies of the Board his flattering reception by Joseph Smith. Remembering this, he hesitated. It would not do to now confess that Mr. Smith had "cut him" on the street. He must pocket the personal indignity and have Mr. Smith return with him, or belittle the imposing figure he had made before the ladies of the Board when describing his reception.

He *could* pocket an indignity; in fact, he *had* done so a hundred times—it was *necessary* in his employment; but he could not belittle the importance of Ezekiel Pelter in the estimation of Board. This he lived on, and he was not so reckless as to fly in the face of his bread and butter.

So, with all his self-importance gone, and with grief and indignation in his heart, he answered:

"They would like to hear something of your *travels*, sir."

"Why, bless their hearts! I would like to please them," John replied; "and I have a little time to spare. How far is it?"

"It's very near," Ezekiel said.

And, with this, they walked along together.

"How did you know me?" inquired John, as they walked along.

"*Know* you!" replied Ezekiel, unable longer to restrain himself. "Did I not *talk* with you?—in—your—own—house?"

"In—my—*house!*" said John deliberately, and looking curiously at Mr. Pelter.

"I wonder if the old chap drinks," was his reflection.

In a little time they reached the rooms.

When the ladies perceived them coming, and heard Ezekiel's well-known voice say, "This way sir," there was a buzzing in the room. Every one was instantly engaged in some new arrangement of her dress, or in fixing on some striking posture, and before the door was opened, all were ready, and apparently engaged in some important work in hand. Of course, they were so much engaged that they did not hear Ezekiel enter, and were much surprised when they saw him in the room, with Mr. Smith beside him; and, of course, one lady cried:

"Oh! Mr. P-e-l-t-e-e-r!"

Then all took notice of the distinguished presence, and the stranger was received in becoming form.

It is to be regretted that Ezekiel felt the chill of his street encounter on him now. Except for this, these pages would be graced by some exalted and inspiring words from him; for there never was a better time than now for him to speak. So it is, that all of us are made to suffer, through a great and good man's injury!

The ladies looked for something from Ezekiel; and Miranda's well was full. But not a touching or a brilliant word did Mr. Pelter utter: he was walking in a cloud, and his thoughts were very, very bitter.

Not even this detracted from his majestic port, and with graceful motions of his hand, he performed the separate introductions.

"How can I serve you, ladies?" was John's first inquiry, when the introductions were concluded.

This broke the spell of awkward silence, and Miranda, moved by her gushing and impulsive nature, quickly answered:

"Oh, sir! tell us of your strange adventures! Of the sights you 've seen! and of the poor, deluded idol-worshipers!"

"Do you pity them?" asked John, turning to the excited maiden.

"O! I do! I do!" exclaimed Miranda.

"Then pity me—and all mankind," said John, with a pleasant, smiling look, and bowing to the gushing vessel.

"What do you mean, sir?" asked Miranda, puzzled, and yet much pleased by his attention.

"All of us are idol-worshipers!" answered John.

"Oh, Mr. Smith! What *do* you mean?" Miranda asked again; feeling strangely fluttered by his smiling look.

"What senseless idols do we worship?" responded John. "You are one of them, and yet seem all unconscious of our adoration!"

Here John bowed, profoundly, with his hand upon his heart, and the look which began to sparkle in his eyes was mistaken for one of tenderness, by the gushing, and now blushing maiden; and she answered—looking rosy as she spoke—by another question:

"And—is it—us you worship?"

Here, the Antique Vessel fairly shone; and John replied—

"Why not?"

Ezekiel was restless and excited now. What did those blushes mean, upon the faded cheeks of his My-*rindy?* The Austere Member was standing by Ezekiel—nearly behind the visitor—and they could hear the conversation with Miranda, and see her flushed and speaking face.

"Did you ever hear such nonsense?" she whispered cautiously in Ezekiel's ear. "See her smirk—and simper—the foolish girl! A pretty looking idol she would make! He's making a fool of her!"

Her feelings would have been quite different, no doubt, had she been standing in Miranda's place.

Beads of perspiration began to start on Ezekiel's face, and as he wiped them off, other beads would quickly form; when the Austere Member spoke to him, the beads began to run in little rills in the wrinkles of his face.

"Is it so warm?" the Austere Member asked, looking at his glowing face. "I had not noticed it."

"I'll make it warm for *him!*" said Ezekiel, spitefully, and glaring on the unconscious John.

"Why, Mr. P-e-l-t-e-e-r!" exclaimed the Member. "Come this way! he will overhear you!"

With this, they drew off together, to another portion of the room. Some of the other members, seeing this, followed after them; and they were soon engaged in low-toned conversation. Soon, other members followed, until Miranda was left alone with the distinguished traveler.

Now, John stooped slightly, and, speaking in a lower tone, inquired:

"Who is that oily chap?"

Miranda, in surprise, replied:

"Who? Mr. P-e-l-t-e-e-r?"

"Yes," said John, "that's what he called himself. Who is he, anyhow?"

"Why, sir," said Miranda, blushing, "he's a member of our Board!"

"Does he drink too much occasionally?" inquired John.

"Oh, Mr. Smith! How can you think so! No!"

"Well, he 's a funny acting fellow then."

"How? What do you mean?"

"Why, he came up to me upon the street, as though he was my brother at the very least, and insisted that he knew me. I tried to correct his evident mistake, and he said that he had visited at my house!"

"Well; so he had."

"He had? For what? To see my wife?"

"To see yourself, sir! He told us all about it; and what you said to him. That 's why we sent him for you."

"He 's a ——— humbug! to draw it mildly. I never saw him in my life before; and he was never at my house!"

"*W-h-a-t?*" was all, in her astonishment, the astounded girl could say.

"It 's all his oily blarney!" continued John; "he never saw me in the world until to-day."

Miranda had never stopped to think that *she* might be an idol-worshiper, and that Ezekiel had been her Joss; but now she felt it, and to see her idol overturned by this strange hand — for the lever of distrust plays havoc with our idols — and to feel the foundations of her faith surely slipping from beneath her, was to be confounded for the moment. But she had a heart of wondrous elasticity, and with an instant for reflection, she invested the destroying hand with supernatural power, and trampling on her prostrate idol she set up a new divinity, in the person of the man before her.

John made a better looking god than Mr. Pelter; and when her mind was turned in his direction, Miranda felt much better satisfied with him. In poetic fancy, she could circumnavigate the globe with John, and fill their sails with aromatic breezes; but Ezekiel was too real, and he would expose his grossness sometimes, in spite of all her ideal drapery.

When a woman makes a change in idols, she feels no sympathy for the one dethroned; and Miranda was a woman.

"What an artful hypocrite he has been!" said she, with a contemptuous look in the direction of Ezekiel. "He made himself of great importance! and told us how he had impressed you! But let him pass. Now, do tell us, Mr. Smith, something of your travels!" Here she gave him such a look as had often thrilled Ezekiel with rapture.

"I have no time for any lengthy talk to-day," said John; "but, perhaps some other time I will amuse you."

"Oh! *will* you, Mr. Smith?" the gushing maiden interrupted.

"But now, in truth," continued John, "I have not the time. Let us see what the ladies wish."

During this brief and harmless conversation the members were in earnest consultation.

John and Miranda, by speaking cautiously, and in a tone inaudible to them, seemed to arouse suspicion, and Miranda's rapturous look was noticed by them all. Perhaps, if left alone, the ladies would not have looked unfavorably on Miranda's evident success in efforts to entertain and please the visitor; but they were not left alone. Ezekiel was there, with the recollection of his street encounter, and with the greater provocation of the traveler's trifling with his adored "My-*rindy*."

"He's a wolf!" Ezekiel exclaimed, in great excitement; "and a godless libertine!—with a *h-u-n*-dred wives—and *c-o-n*-cubines, no doubt! It stands to *reason*, ladies! Why did you send for him? To talk to you, as idols? No! What *then?* To tell My-*rindy* that he worshiped her? No! What THEN? I'll tell you what! To talk of heathen idols—of idols made of wood! and stone! and *such*-like idols! What DID he talk about? Oh, he is the roaring lion mentioned in the Scriptures! Beware of him! Beware of him! and—save—My-*rindy!*"

Here the good man's feelings overpowered him, and he caught the contemptuous glance of his My-*rindy*, and his noble heart stood still.

It was a trying moment for the members of the Board, for Ezekiel's speech and look astonished them.

"What shall we do?" asked one.

"Tell us what to do!" another said.

"What shall we say?" inquired a third.

"Tell us what to say!" exclaimed a fourth.

Ezekiel, now somewhat recovered, was equal to the great occasion.

"Let us confine ourselves to business," he calmly said to them. "We propose to make up supplies for the field in Southern Africa; let us ask him what in his opinion would be most suitable to send."

An approving look was on all the faces of the Board, and here John's repeated inquiry was heard:

"How can I serve you, ladies?"

The Austere Member made the inquiry suggested by Ezekiel.

"Send them blankets!" John replied; "good, warm blankets!"

With a twinkle in his eye, he added to Miranda—speaking in a lower tone—"As well send blankets as anything, for the natives will not get sight of them."

"Blankets for *Africa!*" said the Austere Member, in supreme astonishment.

"*Warm* blankets!" another said.

"Warm blankets for *South* Africa!" exclaimed the others, in a chorus.

Ezekiel was too indignant for expression, but he managed to articulate, very slowly, and with protruding eyes and hands upraised: "*B-l-a-n-*kets—for—South—*Af*-rica!"

In the midst of this sudden consternation, John turned to his companion, and, with a nod and smile, he said "Good day," and disappeared. When the members looked to see what explanation he would offer, his place was vacant, and Miranda stood alone.

Ezekiel was the first to move and speak. He made a headlong rush; breaking through the circle of his saintly friends, and causing them to gaze in some surprise, on his impetuous movements. Stretching out his arms as he approached the maiden, and with his sonorous voice quavering with emotion, he fervently exclaimed: "How often, O My-*rindy!* would I have gathered you together—"

"You need n't mind about it!" said the fickle spinster, interrupting him; and then she drew away.

Here again, a sudden chill congealed his burning eloquence; and he stopped, and dropped his arms, struck by a cruel and unpitying hand.

"You have deceived us!" said Miranda. "You never visited the house of Joseph Smith! He never saw you, until to-day!"

The other members started at this sudden and specific accusation, and could not understand it. Mr. Pelter was, for a moment, staggered by the unexpected blow; but soon his bosom began to heave with indignation. While he hesitated, however, his ardent passion for Miranda restrained hot words of wrath, which else had crushed her, and a look of benignant pity glorified his face.

He spoke, at first, but a single word; but the look of mingled adoration and reproach with which he pointed it, can not be pictured in description. That single word was the one he loved the best of all—

"*My*-RINDY!"

That she could hear that word unmoved, when pronounced in such a tone, and with such a look, was sufficient even for Ezekiel to see that the place he had held in her gushing heart, was closed to him for evermore.

He was fired by this to defensive measures; for he saw as well, that he must acquit himself before the ladies of the Board.

"Did he say that to you, My-*rindy?*—that he did not know me? and that I was never at his house?" asked Mr. Pelter.

"Yes," replied Miranda.

"Now I see it all!" said he, with a look of horror on his face. "O, the artful plot! O, the seductive wiles! First, he tries to estrange you from your friends, by his slandering tongue! Then—what then? O, My-*rindy!* he is a villain! I *do* know him! and I saw him at his house! and we talked together,—as I reported to you all! Can you believe this stranger, and suspicion me?"

"All—this—seems—strange; *ve-ry* strange!" now said the Austere Member. "I can not understand it, Mr. Pelter!"

The loving, lingering accent on his name was gone; and he noticed it: he noticed also, in the member's look, what he had never seen before—an evident distrust. More anxious now than ever, he renewed his protestations.

"I assure you!—upon my honor!—that I speak the truth," said he.

"What motive could he have for denying what you say? His character is high—as you yourself confess—and he is spoken of, by every one, with great respect."

Here Mr. Pelter drew himself up, in his most admired and commanding attitude.

"What *motive*, madam!" continued he. "Were you blind? Could you not see?" Then, turning to Miranda, and pointing to her: "There is the motive! THERE! He would lead that precious soul away, and send it to perdition. That is the motive, madam! And now I see it all!"

"O, you wretch! You deceitful wretch!" cried out Miranda, in hysterical excitement. "You are the one who tries to deceive and tempt me!—You!—*you!*—YOU!" Here, hysteria entirely possessed her; and, with tears and sobs, and some spasmodic jerks, she made a picture quite distressing.

The ladies at once surrounded her, as though to protect her from Ezekiel; but he—poor man—was so stunned, from this last stroke of his My-*rindy*, that he was incapable of offering harm to any one.

Here stood the Moral Paragon! the living proof of charity! deserted and—ALONE! Without the guilt of Adam, he was threatened with expulsion from the moral garden of the Board! But he would not go unheard.

"I will prove to you," said he, "that what I say is true."

With this, he took his broad-brimmed hat and with a heavy, long-drawn sigh, and a lingering look at his adored My-*rindy*, walked sorrowfully away.

CHAPTER III.

RACHEL AND EZEKIEL IN A COMPROMISING SITUATION.

As Mr. Pelter walked sorrowfully away, he reflected on his unjust treatment. A feeling of resentment, unnatural in his tender heart, at once succeeded to his apathetic misery.

He entirely forgot the scriptural injunction, to turn his other cheek, and to forgive his enemies; and, if he had thought of it, it would have seemed to him like a satire on humanity.

He had many times advised this course to others, but it was quite another thing to act on it in his own affairs. In this he was not unlike the majority of those who spend their lives in fitting jackets for their fellows, which they themselves refuse to wear.

With every step his indignation and his anger grew, and by the time he had reached his house a resolute determination had been formed.

His wife observed his unusual look, and she spoke to him in a tone of curious interest. But he did not answer her, and with clouds upon his stately brow, he made his way at once to a private room, where he was accustomed to prepare the reports and official circulars of the Ladies' Board.

While hot with his resentment he commenced to write. Even when his "cross" appeared, and with wondering looks inquired: "What are you at?" he did not answer. He did not even look up, until, in her sharp, commanding voice, she called out:

"*Pelter!*"

Then, for the first time in his life, he replied, with spirit:

"You bother me! Go 'way!"

No wonder that his wife was dazed; or that she yielded in amazement to this assertion of authority; or, that she muttered as she closed the door and went away—

"I could respect him almost, if he could keep up this show of spirit, and not be truckling to that Board of Petticoats!"

There was gall and wormwood on Ezekiel's pen, and thoughts as bitter in his heart. When he had finished writing, he read what he had written, and a calm cold smile of satisfaction succeeded to the blandness on his face.

Slowly and carefully he folded up what he had written. Then he sealed it. Then he wrote the superscription. The superscription was as follows:

Mrs. Joseph Smith,

1647 ——— Street,

City.

With this he hurried out, and before his anger cooled, he put it in the nearest letter-box.

"The villain is unmasked!" he exclaimed; and again he walked away — not sorrowful, but exultant.

On the following day the letter was delivered. Rachel was at home, and she personally received it. She looked at the handwriting. It was strange to her. Then she noticed that it was a city letter; and then she wondered from whom it could have come.

She might have ascertained the fact at first, by looking at the letter; and now, as though that thought had just occurred to her, she opened it. First she read the signature.

"Ezekiel Pelter — who is he?" said she, continuing her self-questioning. "Oh yes, I remember now; he is that pleasant and fine-spoken gentleman who called on Joseph, as a member of the Missionary Board. I wonder if the letter *is* for me; perhaps it is for Joseph."

Here she read the address.

"*Dear Madam*—"

"It is for me. But why should Mr. Pelter write to me?"

After all this questioning, she resolved to read the letter. She soon became so entirely absorbed in it—so painfully absorbed in it—that she changed in every look.

The letter was as follows:

"*Dear Madam, and Sister in the Bonds of Faith:*

"I find myself in a position most painfully embarrassing. I have prayed most earnestly for divine direction, and He appears to make my duty plain to me."

(This opening sentence was one of Mr. Pelter's favorite hyperboles—especially when about to undertake a thing of questionable propriety—and he was so accustomed to its use, that he did not stop to think, that in fact, he had *not* prayed for divine direction; and that if any supernatural spirit prompted him, it was doubtless that of Beelzebub. He found it most convenient, at all such times, to charge his meanness to the Lord, and then take personal credit for his virtues. St. Peter must keep a watchful eye on the celestial gates, or Mr. Pelter will outwit him.) The letter continued:

"What I have to write will prove distressing to you; and *as* I write my heart is bleeding

3

for you." (Another hyperbole of Mr. Pelter's.) "Even now I feel inclined to stop, but duty urges me. A precious soul demands my interference! Shall I be silent, and see that precious soul entrapped by artful snares, until the Evil One shall come and take it to himself? I can not! Shall I not rather, by sounding the alarm, prevent the consummation of the wicked act? Do you inquire how all this concerns yourself? It is my painful duty to inform you.

"It is your husband—Joseph Smith—who leads this lamb of our little flock to the gates of hell! Astonishing as this may seem to you, incredulous as you may be at first, a simple statement of the facts will force conviction on your mind.

"Miranda Trap is the youngest, fairest, and most spiritual member of our Board; and we all watch over her with great solicitude, so impulsive is her nature. She is very precious to our hearts. In an evil hour your husband met her, and he at once began to practice his seductive arts —even saying to her that he 'WORSHIPED' her! —that is the very word. She, an artless child in all her thoughts, was pleased by his attention, and finally she became so thoroughly infatuated that she abandoned her dearest friend for him.

"We must save this precious soul! I write to you, that you may check your husband in his licentious course, and *I* will seek for help and strength in continued prayer.

"Faithfully your friend,

"In Christian sympathy,

"Ezekiel Pelter."

Rachel read the letter with the most astonishing composure, and by the time she had finished it her face was as hard as stone.

Some wives would have been broken by it utterly: most wives would have been so shocked by it as to display profound emotion. But Rachel was only weak in her professions: in her nature she was as hard, and cruel, and pitiless as Fate. Even the wrinkles in her face seemed to set themselves and petrify, when she had finished reading, until they looked like some rough chiseling on a granite form. Without so much as a trembling of her hands, she folded up the letter, and put it in the bosom of her dress. After a moment's silence she, unconsciously, began to speak:

"She was the fairest of the flock, was she? As artless as a child in all her thoughts! The most spiritual among them! Quite a paragon indeed. *I* am *not* fair enough for Joseph, I suppose; nor artless enough! nor spiritual enough! He 'll find me furious enough, if he is n't careful!"

Such thoughts and self-communings did not tend to make Rachel cheerful; as the day passed on, the stony face did not relax; when Joseph entered, at his usual hour, it even seemed to harden more. But the flashes from her eyes were like glints from polished steel.

"What is the matter, Rachel?" asked Joseph, in surprise.

"Humph!" she answered, with a contemptuous motion.

"What *is* it, Rachel? Tell me what it is," insisted Joseph.

"Have you been setting traps to-day?" she spitefully retorted.

"Setting traps! What do you mean?" said he, with growing wonder.

"Trap should be a word familiar to you," answered Rachel. "But perhaps you use the more poetic one, *M-i-r-a-n-d-a!* How is she?"

"Rachel!" now said Joseph, in a tone of sharp rebuke, "explain yourself! What is all this nonsense?"

"Explain myself! That 's good! Ha, ha, ha! How well you play your part! After you — after you, sir, I will explain!"

"After me! And what shall *I* explain?"

"Explain your amours with Miranda Trap!" cried Rachel, with a stormy look. "And if you tell me honestly, everything, even if I hate you,

I will not despise you, as I shall if you try concealment!"

"For Heaven's sake!" cried Joseph, "tell me what it is you're talking of!"

"Then," said Rachel, drawing herself up, "you will not confess! You prefer contempt! O, you canting hypocrite!"

Now, Joseph had been accustomed to command in storms before, though not in such storms as this, but here he was not disposed to shrink, for his patience was exhausted.

"*Leave the room!*" said he; and he spoke as he had spoken on the sea, when the storm was rending all his sails, and his strong-ribbed ship was struggling with the waves. She had never heard this voice before, and in spite of all her courage, she trembled with alarm. She left the room. Some little time elapsed before she regained composure. When she was restored, she reflected on her situation. Of Joseph's guilt she entertained no doubt, and his anger seemed to her a "confirmation strong." But she had not the courage to again provoke his wrath. She resolved to watch with the vigilance of hate, and to consult with Mr. Pelter on the means to be adopted.

Joseph was bewildered. He had no basis even for conjecture. He would have pressed for further explanations had he not already seen that it would be worse than useless. His wife had called him a "canting hypocrite," and this was an offense not to be forgotten.

The evening and the night passed by without a change in the *status belli.* After breakfast on the following morning, Joseph took his hat and walked away, without a word to Rachel. No sooner was he off, than Rachel resolved at once to summon to her aid the valiant Christian soldier of the Board. She sat down and wrote to Mr. Pelter. She urged him to come, as soon as possible; and fixed a time "when," she wrote, "Joseph will be absent, and we will be undisturbed." She signed the letter simply, "Rachel."

She could not expect him sooner than the following day; and with Christian fortitude she engaged herself in her usual household duties.

Now it so happened that Joseph had not been long down town, before he encountered, on the street, the good man Mr. Pelter. Joseph was glad to see him, and, holding out his hand most cordially, he said:

"Good morning, Mr. Pelter. How are the ladies of the Board?"

To Mr. Pelter this seemed like impertinence in the most sublime degree, and he was so indignant that he could scarcely speak. He drew up, and with a flaming face and a voice trembling with passion, said;

"I scorn you, sir!"

Joseph dropped his extended hand at this, and stared at Mr. Pelter. Then his face flamed, and he answered sharply, and with angry eyes:

"What do you mean, sir?"

Ezekiel, not to be intimidated by Joseph's frown, retorted hotly:

"You know what I mean! And I give you notice that I will save My-*rindy* from your licentiousness! For shame, sir! for shame! And you a married man; and with a trusting Christian wife!"

Saying this, Ezekiel passed proudly on, leaving Joseph in fresh mazes of bewilderment.

"*He* talks about this same Miranda!" reflected Joseph. "It seems as though there was a Trap, somewhere! but it is set too cunningly for me. I never heard of such a person as Miranda Trap. Some vicious scamp has put this up on me. I don't suppose there is such a person as Miranda Trap! It's hard to fight such shadows. I must make Rachel explain it to me!"

While engaged in these reflections, Joseph, too, was passing on; but all the noises and bustle of the street did not drive away this mysterious specter — Miranda Trap.

That night, the atmosphere at home had a smell of brimstone, and Joseph thought it prudent to postpone his questions to his wife until it cleared somewhat. The following morning was not clear, and Joseph thought that he would leave the matter for another day; or, at least, till he came home to dinner.

That morning was an exciting and eventful one to Mr. Pelter. Rachel's letter came. He read it with peculiar satisfaction, but he did not speak, for his wife was in the room.

"Who's the letter from?" she asked.

"Oh—it's a business matter," answered Mr. Pelter.

"That's not what I want to know. Who is it from?"

"No matter, no matter," answered Mr. Pelter, getting nervous, and putting the letter in the inner pocket of his coat.

"No matter, eh?" replied his virtuous spouse; and then she rose, with resentment in her face, and left the room.

"Wife!" called out Mr. Pelter, presently; and she came back. "I wish you would sew a button on my coat," said he.

His coat was off, and he was engaged in dressing, with unusual care. She took it in her hand, and asked: "Is the button all?"

"Yes," he answered.

She went out again, taking Ezekiel's coat. No sooner had the door closed after her than she put her hand in the inner pocket and drew out

Rachel's letter. She put it in the pocket of her dress, with a look of satisfaction, and then sat down to sew the button on. When she returned the coat, she asked: "Are you going out?"

"Yes," he answered; and he was very restless; for it would be a sorry day for him if his spirited companion should discover his unlawful passion for Miranda Trap.

So, being restless, and dreading further questions, he finished dressing as soon as possible, and without thinking of the letter, took his broad-brim hat and went away.

When he had gone, his wife took Rachel's letter from her pocket and sat down to read it. The letter was as follows:

"*My dear Mr. Pelter:*

"Ever since I received your letter I have been burning with a desire to see you——"

"This letter then," said Mrs. Pelter, "is not the first! 'burning—with—desire!'" But she was too impatient for another word, and continued reading.

"My husband will be away from home all day to-morrow——"

"Ah!" cried the jealous wife; but still she read.

"You *must* come soon! and you had better come when Joseph is away, and we will be undisturbed——"

"Oh, the shameless thing!" exclaimed the furious Mrs. Pelter; but still she read:

"O! Joseph was so angry. You must tell me what to do! I am half distracted, and can scarcely wait for you! Do not fail to come—and soon! Your precious 'lamb' must not be forgotten." That was all, except the signature—"Rachel."

"His lamb!" cried Mrs. Pelter, in a rage. "Oh, if I only had her here! This is the sort of missionary work my husband is engaged in! I'll serve his 'lamb' with caper sauce! and they'll be curious capers, too, if I get hold of her! O, wont I?—*wont* I?—WONT I?"

Mr. Pelter, all unconscious of the furious storm gathering behind him, hurried on with eager steps to the house of Joseph Smith. Rachel was waiting for him.

"Oh, Mr. Pelter," she exclaimed, as soon as they were alone together. "What shall I do?"

"Compose yourself, dear lady," said Ezekiel, in his sweetest tone of consolation. "All of us are worms; but we have a Helper."

"I know it Mr. Pelter," Rachel cried; "but, somehow, my religion seems to fit other people's cases better than my own. This is AWFUL!"

"It is, indeed," replied Ezekiel; "but with proper circumspection we may defeat his wicked purposes."

"Oh, I hope so, Mr. Pelter! I hope so! But to think that Joseph could be guilty of such a thing! I have lost all faith in men!"

"Do not say that! do not, I pray you!" And here Ezekiel gave her such a glance as Miranda never could resist.

It did begin to look as though Mr. Pelter, compelled to abandon the moral garden of the Board, was trying now to cultivate the moral garden of Mr. Joseph Smith.

"Well," said Rachel, hesitating, "I will except yourself."

"Thank you, madam; thank you!" said Ezekiel. And here they were interrupted by a servant bringing in some letters which the postman had just left. Rachel took the letters and looked them over; and Ezekiel, who was standing by, let his eyes fall upon them as she looked them over. Soon he stopped her suddenly, saying:

"They are in correspondence!"

"Who?" asked Rachel, looking up.

"Your husband and My-*rindy!*" replied Ezekiel, in profound astonishment.

"What do you mean?" cried Rachel in distress.

"There is a letter from My-*rindy!*" said Ezekiel; and he pointed to the letters in Rachel's hand. "I have seen her write a thousand times, and know her writing."

Rachel, with feverish anxiety, ran the letters over, and soon found one in a woman's hand.

"Is that it?" she asked, holding up the letter.

"It is," said Mr. Pelter.

"What shall I do?" asked Rachel.

Ezekiel had read the story of the monkey and the chestnuts, and he answered promptly: "Open it." He was anxious to see this correspondence.

"I do not dare to open it! I never thought of doing such a thing! Joseph would be very angry!"

"It is your duty, madam. Let him see that he is detected and he will not dare to take another step! Besides, the letter will probably disclose how far they've gone already."

"O, what shall I do?"

"Open it!"

"I am sorely tempted!"

"Do it!"

With trembling hands and fluttering heart she did it. This is what she saw, and she read it to Ezekiel:

"*Mr. Smith, my dear and valued friend:*—

"I do not blame you for it—oh no! I can not find it in my heart to blame you—but—I am—unhappy."

"Poor child!" said Mr. Pelter.

"O, Joseph!" Rachel wailed. But she continued reading:—

"Your words and looks have opened up such new and sweet delights as to fill my heart. Oh for the wings of a dove! that I might fly away from all my trials to the enchanting scenes where you have been!"

"Oh! oh! oh!" cried Rachel.

"O-o-o-o!" groaned Mr. Pelter.

"But," continued Rachel, reading, "I must tell you of my troubles. Mr. Pelter—the odious man!—"

"What? what's that?" exclaimed Ezekiel.

"The odious man!" repeated Rachel, reading.

"Oh, she's lost! she's lost!" cried Mr. Pelter.

"And where is Joseph?" cried the sorrowing Rachel. But still she read:—

"Mr. Pelter—the odious man!—has already turned suspicion on us. I know that you did not intend to place me in a position of such embarrassment,—but you have. When people question me, what can I say? I never will confess the truth, but I fear in spite of me, my face tells something. I will explain what you are charged with, if you will write to me, and tell me when and where I can have a meeting with you. Do write to me—I pray you—soon!

"May God and all his angels bless you, is the prayer of your sorrowing

"MIRANDA."

"O, Mr. Pelter!" burst out Rachel. "What shall I do with this damning proof of Joseph's guilt? She will not confess the truth, she says, but her face tells something! What does it tell? A virtuous woman's face tells nothing to her injury! O, Mr. Pelter!"

Ezekiel was not a fickle man, and without great provocation he would not falter in his allegiance; especially when his bread and butter hung on his fidelity. But the most loyal and magnanimous of men may be driven to revolt.

That word "odious" in Miranda's letter was too much for Mr. Pelter; it pierced his noble heart and made him desperate.

"Your husband mêt My-*rindy* first in the presence of the Ladies' Board," said he. "They encouraged him, and I protested!"

In his sudden indignation he determined to renounce Miranda and all the Missionary Board, and to espouse the cause of the injured Rachel. Impetuous in his zeal — too impetuous, perhaps, and yet displaying in the act his generous and unselfish nature — he fell upon his knees before this new object of his solicitude, and clasped his hands and lifted his sympathizing eyes to hers.

"For heaven's sake get up!" cried Rachel, shocked.

He did not get up, but placed his hands upon

"Impetuous in his zeal, he fell upon his knees before this new object of his solicitude."

his spotless waistcoat, and exclaimed in dramatic tones:

"Lay your troubles on this *boo*-som, Rachel!"

He did not know that a witness stood behind him in the open door, but Rachel's eyes were full of fear, for she saw her husband standing there.

Joseph heard Ezekiel's last dramatic speech, and he stopped to hear no more. Quickly stepping up behind him, he took Ezekiel by the ear and dragged him howling to his feet; still holding on, he gave a sudden jerk and forced Ezekiel toward the door, then by a dexterous movement of his foot he sent the good man flying through the door. All this was done without a spoken word; then Joseph took Ezekiel's broad-brim hat and threw it after him.

Ezekiel was a man of courage; but it was a spiritual courage—his flesh was weak. He quickly grasped his broad-brim hat, and with a frightened look behind, to see if Joseph followed, he hastened to the outer door; then he rushed out, and made such progress down the street as astonished all beholders.

Were these not veracious chronicles this scene might be omitted, for it is the darkest cloud upon Ezekiel's long and useless life; charity, which had sheltered him so long, should cover it as well.

Joseph turned on Rachel with such a look of fury as made her cower. She began to utter protestations, but he stopped her.

"This," said he, "explains itself; don't make it worse by attempting to excuse yourself!"

Rachel sank into a chair, completely overcome.

Joseph began pacing back and forth across the room. At length he stopped before his wife, and asked:

"Where did you pick up that man?"

"O, Joseph—" she commenced.

"Stop!" he cried. "No excuses, if you please! How—came—he—here?"

"I sent for him."

"You sent for him! Then you're the one that's setting traps!"

Rachel here plucked courage from the letter in her hand, and with a bolder front she answered:

"Not setting traps, but finding what is caught in them!"

"What do you mean by that?"

"You are in the trap; and I have caught you, sir!"

"Don't try to draw me off! Explain the amorous scene I witnessed here!"

"Sir!" replied the virtuous Rachel, rising up. "I scorn your base insinuation!"

"You 'scorn' it, do you? Why you have his very form of speech! He said, 'I scorn you, sir!' But I am waiting for your explanation."

"You said the matter explained itself! First, you explain! Explain — that — letter!"

Here, quivering with excitement, she held out to him Miranda's letter. He took the letter from her hand and looked at it.

"Who opened this?" he asked.

"I did!" she answered boldly.

"And do you employ my correspondence for the entertainment of your lover?"

This cut Rachel like a lash, and nearly wild she cried:

"You shall not insult me by such language!"

"I beg your pardon," said Joseph, with a bow and sneer. "Will you lay your troubles on my '*boo*-som,' Rachel? This, I find, is the proper form of speech."

Rachel felt the lash again, but again she advanced to the attack.

"See what troubles you have laid in the bosom of Miranda Trap! Read that letter!"

"'Still harping on my daughter,' are you?" With this, he commenced to read the letter.

"What's this?" said he, looking up at her.

"Oh, how in-no-cent!" said she.

He looked at the envelope to be sure of the address, and then at the signature.

"Miranda Trap again!" said he. "Why, woman, I never saw or heard of such a person as Miranda Trap! What is it all?"

"Oh, Joseph, Joseph! do not stain your soul by falsehood! It 's bad enough as 't is; do n't make it worse, as you said to me just now."

"Falsehood! I speak the truth!"

"Do you forget who saw you when you met her first? Or, are you calculating on my ignorance?"

"Who says I ever met her?"

"Mr. Pelter."

"Do n't dare to speak his name again!"

"Well, then, all the ladies of the Missionary Board saw you Joseph, and you doubtless thought me ignorant of this."

"I never saw the ladies of the Missionary Board!"

"Oh, Joseph! how can you tell me that?"

"Do n't you believe me?"

"I wish I could believe you."

"Will you believe what they say, then? If they tell you so, will you believe it?"

"Yes."

"Very well; I 'll leave you no excuse for your *dis*belief. I 'll see if I can find these ladies, and agree upon a time to meet. Now let me have your explanation of the scene I witnessed here just now."

"I will explain, and to your perfect satisfaction, if you will wait until we see the ladies of the Board."

"What has that to do with this?"

"It has everything to do with it! It will furnish you a key, without which you cannot understand me."

"All this is beyond my comprehension. This is not a matter to be trifled with; and I tell you, Rachel, if you do not make your innocence appear, this will be a sorry day for you."

"My innocence will appear, and I only ask for this delay that it may be clear to you."

"Well, well, I'll wait; you shall have the advantage of the key."

"And, Joseph, don't forget that you must make your innocence appear."

"As to this Miranda Trap?"

"Yes."

"That is a very easy matter."

"I hope so."

"I know so! You did not expect me in this morning?"

"No."

"Had you, I should have missed the sight of your carpet-knight, no doubt."

"You agreed to leave that subject for the present."

"And so I will. I came back to get some papers that I need. I will get them and be off. I will try to see the ladies of the Board while I am out."

Here Joseph left the room to find his papers, and very soon he left the house.

When Mr. Pelter had placed a sufficient distance between himself and Joseph Smith, he attempted to resume his usual stately walk and mien. It was impossible. His great heart throbbed with grief unspeakable. No more, for him, the sweet and cheap delights of charity! No more bouquets, or choice perfumes, from that moral garden where he used to snuff the odorous air! No more companionship with the congenial spirits of the Ladies' Board! His glory had departed, and even his "My-*rindy*" had called him ODIOUS!"

If Alexander wept for other worlds to conquer — and it was a very silly thing to do — would he not have fairly howled if he had lost by one sharp stroke of fate all the teeming worlds over which Ezekiel had held his gentle sway? That broad domain extended, as Ezekiel used to sing,

> "From Greenland's icy mountains
> To India's coral strand."

But Hope would not desert him utterly, and she sent a glint from her flickering lamp. Would not Rachel lay her troubles on his "*boo*-som," and fill the aching void beneath his waistcoat? Living on this slender, single hope, he proceeded sadly to his house. He entered, and retired to his favorite room. He should have kept away from there, for too many recollections of his departed glory were suggested by the strange and miscellaneous contents of that little room.

Here were tracts, and circulars, and charity appeals — all the coinage of his cunning brain — strewn in disorder on his table. Now, they seemed to him like dead, inodorous flowers on a grave of buried hopes.

It was too much: and in an agony of spirit which convulsed his frame, he sat down and stretching his arms upon the table, bowed his head upon them, and with a groan surrendered to despair.

While thus contending with emotion, he heard a voice — a familiar voice — and one most painfully distinct.

The voice cried, "*Pelter!*"

What a harsh and jangling discord in the bitter-sweets of Ezekiel's memories! He slowly raised his head and looked around. There stood his wife — his "cross" — with sleeves rolled up and fury blazing in her eyes. Her sleeves were not rolled up with reference to any pugilistic exercise, but because she was engaged in the unromantic labors of her "washing."

"Do I look like a woman to be trifled with?" she asked.

"No, indeed!" Ezekiel answered, with a sudden quake of fear. Nor did she look like a woman to be trifled with.

Then she stepped briskly forward, and before Ezekiel could recover from astonishment, she bundled up his tracts, and circulars, and charity appeals, and all his precious manuscripts, and took them from the room. She was not long away. When she returned, Ezekiel asked what she had done with them.

"They 're ashes!" was the furious answer.

Ezekiel groaned.

"Now," said Mrs. Pelter, "I want to have a talk with you! Tell me first, who is Rachel?"

As quick as thoughts could flash, they pointed Mr. Pelter to the letter so carefully concealed. By an involuntary motion, his hand rested on the pocket where he had placed it. It was gone.

"You needn't look for that!" said she; "I have the letter. Who is she? I ask."

Ezekiel's ideas of moral duty, as he had expounded them to Rachel when he urged her to read what was not intended for her eye, were coming home to roost; and now he really held quite different views. But he did not state them. He thought it best to answer Mrs. Pelter.

"She is Mrs. Smith," said he, now quite subdued.

"What Mrs. Smith?"

"Mrs. Joseph Smith."

"Is she a member of your Board of Holy Petticoats?"

"No."

"What did she want of you?"

"She wanted to consult with me."

"What about?"

"Some trouble with her husband."

"I-n-d-e-e-d! And did you console her?"

"She had been much abused, and I felt sorry for her."

"Good man! Did you console her?"

"Well, yes; I trust I gave her help."

"Now, Pelter! I find that by helping heathen and your neighbors' wives, you are so much occupied that your own house sees but little of you. From this time out, I shall give these ladies notice that *I* must have your help. I think, upon the whole, that I shall advise you to have less to do with other peoples' wives, and more with your own.

"Oh," cried Mr. Pelter, anxiously, "the ladies will not trouble you again."

"What? Is that what troubles you? Have they sent you adrift at last to get an honest living? Are there no more crumbs for the saintly Mr. P-e-l-t-e-e-r? Then come with me; I'll show you how you can be useful!"

"What do you want with me?" asked the poor man dazed.

"I'll show you; come along."

He followed her until they reached the kitchen.

"Do you see that pile of clothes?" she asked, pointing to the washing in a tub.

"Of course I see it," said Ezekiel.

"Well, take off your coat and help me with them."

"Help — you — w-a-s-h!"

"Yes! You've washed more dirty linen in your Board than you'll find here! Shall I help you with your coat?"

Saying this, she took hold of Ezekiel's coat, and in spite of all his protestations, soon had it off.

"Now let me tie this apron on," she said; and she took a long and faded apron, and tied it on, then placed him by the tub, and showed him how to turn the wringer, while she supplied it.

CHAPTER IV.

MR. PELTER IS AGAIN A JOSS.

JOSEPH sent over to the rooms of the Ladies' Board, as soon as he had ascertained where they could be found, and asked if they could fix an early day to receive himself and wife. The ladies were unusually excited when the messenger arrived, but they consulted for a moment and fixed upon the following day. The messenger then retired, and reported their conclusion.

The unusual excitement in the Board when the messenger arrived was caused by the report of a committee just returned from the discharge of an important duty. The report cannot be fully comprehended without a circumstantial detail of the action of the Board in relation to it.

After Mr. Pelter had retired, leaving Miranda in hysterics, as related in a former chapter, the ladies began to clear the moral atmosphere. It was determined, from the first, that Miranda Trap was the unconscious victim of some infamous design. It had not occurred to them till now that Mr. Pelter might be the guilty man.

Miranda had distinctly charged him with trying to "deceive" and "tempt" her. What did she mean by this? And what did Mr. Pelter mean by his references to Joseph Smith?

Here was a better field for microscopic search than they had had of late, and they determined to improve the opportunity. They began by questioning Miranda — she still indulging in a copious overflow of tears.

"Now, Miranda," said the Austere Member, let us hear your explanation. What did you mean by charging Mr. Pelter with trying to 'deceive' and 'tempt' you?"

With interjected sobs, Miranda answered, "He — has — deceived — us — all!"

"How?" "How?" "How?"

Inquired the different members of the Board.

"By pretending that he knew Joseph Smith, and telling us about a pretended interview with him. This is false! He never saw him until to-day! And if he would falsify in this, would he not in other things?"

"True;" "True;" "True;" replied the members of the Board.

"But how do you know that this was false?" asked the Austere Member.

"Why, Mr. Smith said it was," replied Miranda, "and he said that Mr. Pelter was a hypocrite!"

This was a serious charge indeed, and it caused serious looks upon the faces of the Board.

"How has he tried to 'tempt' you?" continued the Austere Member, now with stern judicial gravity.

"In *ev*-ery way!" sobbed Miranda. "He has tried to secure my af-*fec*-tions! And — oh, forgive me, ladies, for I had no thought of wrong — he — did!"

With this confession she broke down, and all the members raised their hands in horror.

To say that the Board was shocked by this disclosure, is to convey but a very faint impression of the real sensation.

"She is so impulsive!" one remarked.

"Poor child!" another said.

"And he a married man!" a third exclaimed.

"We should have kept a better watch on him," was the judicial comment of the Austere Member. And abuse rained down upon the imaginary head of Mr. Pelter, sufficient, had it fallen on his actual head, to have crushed him utterly. They were so indignant that, for the moment, they forgot the peculiar conduct of Mr. Smith. Miranda was a victim. This, in itself, was a great point gained by her. It did not occur to one of them to inquire how far Miranda's gushing passion was in fault, and whether, after all, Ezekiel was not more sinned against than sinning.

Miranda, under this strong support of sympathy, very soon recovered; and as a victim, she was actually caressed by all the members of the Board.

"And this," said one, "is why he was so furióus at Mr. Smith!"

"Oh yes! I had forgotten Mr. Smith," said the Austere Member. "Tell us what he said to you, Miranda."

Miranda told them what he said; but not how she had received it, or how she looked at him.

"In this there was nothing in the least improper," was the verdict of the Board: "but why did he make that ridiculous suggestion as to blankets for South Africa? And why did he run away so suddenly?"

Miranda laughed—a genuine laugh—at this, and then explained that it was but a bit of pleasantry in Mr. Smith, and that he was obliged to go away; so he had told her.

"But," said Miranda, "he told me he would come again some other day, and give you any information he was able to."

So Miranda spurned her broken idol, and excused her new divinity; order was restored and the moral atmosphere was cleared. Mr. Smith was vindicated and Ezekiel doomed.

After this, by formal vote, Mr. Pelter was indefinitely suspended from the Board, and a committee was appointed to notify the fallen man. The committee fixed upon the day of Ezekiel's visit to the distracted Rachel for their official visit. They had often been at Mr. Pelter's house before, and the good man usually appeared from his little room, to receive and welcome them. Expecting now that he would answer it, they rang the bell.

The tinkle reached the kitchen, and suspended operations there.

"The bell!" cried Mr. Pelter, with the handle of the wringer in his hand.

"I'll answer it," said Mrs. Pelter, and she started for the door.

"Tell them that I am out!—left the city!—dead!" cried Mr. Pelter after her; but she was out of hearing.

"Is Mr. P-e-l-t-e-e-r in?" inquired the committee.

"He is," said Mrs. Pelter, very stiffly. "Would you like to see him?"

"If you please," the committee answered.

"Step this way," said Ezekiel's "cross."

She led them to the kitchen, opened the kitchen door, and stood aside for them to enter. They stopped upon the threshold, speechless with amazement. There stood Ezekiel!—the Moral

Paragon! — the broken monument of Charity! — standing by the wash-tub and perspiring in the rising steam.

Red as he was from the unaccustomed exercise, he was redder still from shame, when he looked down and saw his long and faded apron. In a sudden frenzy, which for the moment was superior to any fear of consequences, he tore the apron off and trampled on it. Then, with greater dignity, he took his coat and put it on, and with his lofty and commanding bow and gesture to the members of the Board, walked proudly from the kitchen.

Mrs. Pelter saw that for the moment her authority was gone, and without a word she saw Ezekiel escort the ladies to his little room.

Here the scene was too affecting for description. The little room looked cheerless now, for its sun was veiled: the familiar table was as empty as light promises: the tracts, and circulars, and charity appeals were nowhere to be seen!

"Where are your documents?" inquired one, with a sad and pitying look at the empty table.

There was a look of injured innocence on Ezekiel's face, as he replied:

"Where are all my 'good deeds past?'

'Devour'd
As fast as made! Forgot as soon as done!'"

"Ezekiel was standing by the wash-tub and perspiring in the rising steam."

"No, no! Do not say that!" said the previous speaker; and the ladies began to melt. Ezekiel noticed this, and was quick to take advantage of it. Clasping his hands, and with a peculiar motion of his lips, familiar to provincial favorites in high tragedy — a sort of tragic slobbering — he fairly crushed them with a sense of their ingratitude.

"And now," said he, in closing his masterly appeal to their emotions. "You see the inglorious end of all my willing services! Wringing clothes at a dirty wash-tub!"

With this, his feelings seemed to overpower him, for he sank down into a chair, and bowed his head upon the table. It was a scene to make the very gods look down in pity. Afterward, in describing it, the committee said that they were so overwhelmed that they could think of nothing but Ezekiel's misery.

With tearful eyes, a melted member asked: "Why did you tell us, Mr. Pelter, that you knew Joseph Smith, and had seen him at his house?"

"Because I did and had!" said Mr. Pelter, raising his head. "He denies it that he may discredit me! And why! Because I know his wicked purposes, and am determined to defeat them!"

"What purposes?" the committee asked.

"His designs upon My-*rindy!*" said Ezekiel, rising up in great excitement.

"But that has been explained; there was really nothing in it."

"Who says so?"

"Miranda."

"From bad to worse! From bad — to — worse!"

"What do you mean?"

"Why she has begun to practice what she learned from him!"

"What?"

"Deception!"

"How?"

"She is in correspondence with him — now! and in language of a peculiar character. Amorous, some would call it. She asks him to fix a time and place for a private meeting, and tells him that I have turned suspicion on them. And that though she 'll not confess, she fears her face tells something. And, for all my efforts in her behalf, she calls me O-D-I-O-U-S!"

"Why, Mr. P-e-l-t-e-e-r, this is impossible! it is too shocking! Who told you this?"

"I saw her letter!"

"Where?"

"In the hands of Rachel Smith!"

"The wife of Joseph Smith?"

"His most unhappy wife!"

"And you say that you did know him, and did call on him as you represented?"

"Most assuredly I did!"

This information and these serious charges were too startling to be acted on without a consultation. While they consulted, Mr. Pelter stood with folded arms; and now he first noticed his jealous wife, standing just within the door.

"A pretty lot, the whole of you!" said she, as she caught Ezekiel's eye. "I told you that your Board had more dirty linen to be washed than my kitchen held! Now tell these moral scavengers about your precious letter—and amorous too—from this dear, unhappy Rachel Smith!"

With this she seemed to scent infection in the air, for she turned up her nose and quitted the room.

The committee turned to Mr. Pelter, and one of them inquired: "What is that?—the letter she speaks of?—from Mrs. Smith?"

Mr. Pelter was embarrassed. After a moment's hesitation, he replied:

"My wife—you know—is—pe-culiar."

The tone and look with which he spoke were more significant than the spoken words. They smiled and nodded, as if to say, "We understand; she makes these foolish statements simply to annoy you."

Then Mr. Pelter smiled, for he felt assured that he was re-established in their confidence.

"Now, Mr. P-e-l-t-e-e-r," said a member of the committee, "we have concluded to give you an opportunity to confound your enemies and put them to confusion. We will arrange some way for Mr. Smith to meet the Board again; you will be there, and in presence of us all you can confront, and, if possible, expose him."

At first Ezekiel was very far from pleased with this arrangement, for the weakness of his flesh was a very heavy drag upon his valiant spirit. Then he considered that he would be safe from injury in the presence of the Board; and with this reflection, he replied that nothing could please him more.

So they parted: Ezekiel with reviving hope, and the committee with the sad reflection that Miranda was the guilty one.

It was the return and report of this committee that caused the unusual excitement when the messenger from Joseph Smith appeared before the Board. They reported privately; that is, they informed the members individually of what they had discovered; and every member was informed except Miranda. The conclusion was, that on the following day, when Mr. Smith was present, and Ezekiel and Miranda in attendance, they would investigate, and fix the guilt where it properly belonged.

It seemed as though Ezekiel now would step

into Miranda's niche, and she be tumbled out of it. So uncertain is the foothold of our idols.

On the following day, when the Board convened, there was a look of some anxiety on all their faces; but on the faces of Ezekiel and Miranda it was most marked. Ezekiel could not feel exactly comfortable when he thought of meeting Joseph Smith, and his ear would burn in spite of him: while Miranda could only bear the chilly atmosphere which surrounded her by drawing on the fires of her passion for the expected visitor.

Joseph Smith at length arrived, accompanied by Rachel. The members all rose up and bowed; then Joseph bowed. Mr. Pelter was the only one he had ever seen before; and Mr. Pelter he did not deign to notice. Ezekiel flushed at this, and the ladies seemed surprised. Miranda's heart was in such a flutter that she could not restrain her mounting blushes; and when Joseph looked in her direction, she gave him such a smile as made him pause and look at her attentively. But his look was cold and curious—nothing like the smiling look of John. Her gushing heart grew heavy as she noticed this, and the meteors all disappeared from her flaming face, and left it pale and anxious.

"I beg your pardon for this intrusion, ladies," Joseph commenced; "but I am anxious to clear up, if possible, some strange mistakes and misunderstandings."

Curiosity was now alert, and every ear erect. "Is there such a person present," he continued, "as Miranda Trap?"

Now the meteors tilted in Miranda's face again, and then they died away and left it paler than before.

"You know her," replied the Austere Member, in astonishment, "and must know that she is present."

Here Rachel's look was keen, and she threw a sharp, quick glance at Mr. Pelter.

"Pardon me," said Joseph, with a bow, "but I never saw her in my life. Will you introduce me, or point her out to me?"

"This is ridiculous!" said an indignant member; and she was interrupted by Miranda, who cried out in real distress:

"O, Mr. Smith! this is too much! too cruel in you! And that, too, after all you said to me! O-o-o-o!"

Every one but Joseph felt quite touched by this wail of agony, and even Rachel looked on her with pity, and on him with evident contempt.

"You, then, are Miranda Trap!" said Joseph, turning to her.

"You know I am! you wicked and deceitful

man!" cried the outraged maiden, in a furious tempest of passion.

"I am very glad to find you," said Joseph, calmly, but evidently confused, "for I have been fighting shadows long enough. Now, let me ask you why you wrote this letter to me?"

Here he held out the letter read by Rachel and Ezekiel. Ezekiel groaned.

"O — you — wretch!" now fairly shrieked the furious maiden. "You shall not expose the feelings of my heart in this cruel, cruel way!"

With a panther's bound she sprung to him, and caught the letter from his hand. The Austere Member's face was hard and rigid now, and Rachel's had the chiseled look of the day before.

Joseph was more bewildered every instant, and in actual desperation he commenced again.

"Now, ladies, answer me this question, will you? I ask it to satisfy my wife. She insists that I have been here before, and, that I here met Miranda Trap. I want you, at least, to clear me in this respect. Did you ever see me here before?"

"Yes!" "Yes!" "Yes!" came in various keys of indignation from nearly every member of the Board.

Joseph was dumbfounded.

"Mr. Smith!" began the Austere Member, with her severest look, "if you have compromised yourself with this foolish and impulsive girl, and now attempt to satisfy your wife by this bold repudiation, do not come to us to aid you in your base deception! You should have known us better than to think that we could be employed as instruments in such a sinful thing. You know that you were here, and that you met Miranda here. We know it to our sorrow! Fortunately for her your designs have been unmasked. Except for Mr. Pelter here — and he has suffered for his noble conduct" (here she waved her hand toward Mr. Pelter) — "you might yet be leading this thoughtless and imprudent girl to ruin!"

This public recognition of his services caused Ezekiel's heart to fairly dance within him; and he rose up, and with his hand upon his waistcoat, bowed profoundly.

"I have seen an exhibition of Mr. Pelter's 'noble conduct,'" said Joseph, with a sneer, "and he no doubt preserves a lively recollection of it. I warn him now, and here, to be very careful, or he will not get off so well again."

Ezekiel's fleshly weakness here caused him to tremble, but when he heard a member say:

"Hear him threaten! Mr. Pelter has too many friends!" his reviving spirits nerved his legs, and he stood firm.

"Then you have seen Mr. Pelter!" cried the

Austere Member. "When you were here before you said you had never seen him."

"I never said so! I never even spoke of him!" said Joseph, hotly; "and, as I have already told you, I was never here before!"

Then he turned to Rachel, in his sore perplexity, and asked:

"Is this a mad-house? Or, am *I* demented?"

He only met a cold, hard smile on Rachel's face, and she replied:

"This was to be your test! Are you satisfied?"

"No!" he thundered.

"I AM!" said she. "You are a guilty man! What Mr. Pelter said of you has been here confirmed! He proved a truer friend to me than you!"

Here Mr. Pelter began to swell again, with self-approval, for even his *questionable* acts began to look like virtues. Had Rachel really lain upon his "*boo*-som," perhaps, in some mysterious way, that would have proved the crowning virtue of them all. Such thoughts were very comforting.

Now, this cold, hard woman, who turned upon her husband with a front of stone, crossed over to Miranda with a look of gentle pity in her eyes. She put her hand on Miranda's head, in a caressing way, and said to her:

"Poor child! I am very sorry for you. You have been cheated in a dream — and it was not a virtuous dream, I fear — who can tell? — God knows — but in a little time you will recover, and even be the better for the lesson. *I* have been cheated of my very life, and cannot recover! or—ever—be—the better—for it! God help us all — and pity — ME!"

This was all so sudden, so unexpected, and so majestic in its simplicity, that every one was filled with a reverential awe. Then Rachel turned and said: "Good ladies, I thank you for your frankness, and for your refusal to assist a guilty man in his deceptions."

Without another word to any one, and without looking at her husband, she walked away. Joseph rushed wildly after her.

For a moment after they had gone, no one spoke a word. Had an angel suddenly appeared among them, and rebuked them for their everlasting search for something to condemn, they could not have been more thoroughly astonished than when they saw this stern-faced woman encourage virtue by lessons from our frailties, and then pity and forgive, where she had cause for hatred.

There were chords in Rachel's heart — as there are in every one's, however rough the instrument may look — which, when touched by skillful fingers, will discourse the sweetest harmonies. They were the chords of love and charity, with which the Soul of Harmony strings all our hearts, and when we find them jangling out of tune it is because our hands have tried to change their perfect key.

It was well for the now crushed and penitent Miranda that such chords were struck, for their vibrations reached, and set in corresponding motion, like chords among her fellows. Ezekiel was among the first to feel the pulse; and his heart flew open with a sudden gush of Pelterean charity. Now blandness settled on his face, with a brighter shimmer, and Ezekiel was "himself again."

Miranda, taking courage from his look, felt her heart thrill, and in a penitential voice she cried: "O, forgive me, Mr. P-e-l-t-e-e-r!"

What could Mr. Pelter do but step up to her, and with his hands above her head, in an attitude of benediction, say: "Behold, how good and how pleasant it is for brethren to dwell together in unity!"

From this nettle of distrust the Board thus plucked the flower of harmony, and in Miranda's impulsive heart, Ezekiel was again a Joss, all spangled with her tears of penitence.

CHAPTER V.

VIRTUOUS ZEAL LEADS MR. PELTER INTO DANGER.

WHEN John returned from his visit to the Board, he related to his wife his curious experience. His striking pictures of Mr. Pelter and Miranda were particularly admired; and they served with Julia, for many a day, as targets for her fun. Not long after this, and soon after the exciting incidents just related, Ezekiel and Miranda were on the street together, on some good work of charity.

John and Julia were also on the street that day, and it so happened that they met each other. Julia recognized the missionary twain from John's description; and with laughing eyes she called John's attention to them.

They were looking in *their* direction, and there seemed to be a look of horror on their faces. John stopped, and bowed, and smiled, but the twain did not seem inclined to stop. Miranda, blushing first, then growing pale, turned her face away; and Ezekiel stared, but he stared at Julia, and did not deign to notice John.

" He 's got another *Woo* - man."

As they passed, John heard Ezekiel say: "He 's got another *woo*-man!"

Julia heard him, too, and she quickly asked: "What 's that John? He says you 've got another woman."

John only laughed, and said, "They seem to be offended."

"Why," continued Julia, "the fair Miranda would not even look at you."

"And Mr. Pelter *did* look at you," said John.

"What made her color so, and seem so much confused and fluttered?"

"I do n't know."

"It 's very queer!" persisted Julia; then, looking squarely in her husband's face, she added: "John, you hav' n't been talking nonsense to that girl, have you?"

"Why, no!" said John. "What are you thinking of?" So the subject dropped: by John to be forgotten; by Julia to be stored away in her place for curiosities.

When Ezekiel and Miranda returned to the ladies' rooms, they had a new sensation for the Board. It was opportune; for their "fields" were very sterile now, and they longed for occupation.

"Another one!" exclaimed an excited member, after Mr. Pelter had finished his account of the street encounter, with apt embellishments of speech.

"What next?" exclaimed another.

"How did she look?" inquired a third.

This was the question of substantial interest to all, and they waited for Ezekiel's answer.

"Well—she was fine-looking!" said Ezekiel: and he spoke with kindling eyes and watering mouth,—like children, sometimes, when they talk of luscious peaches. "I may say *splen*-did!" he continued, after, in imagination, another taste.

"Perhaps it was an acquaintance merely," suggested one, in a regretful tone; as though they might be cheated after all, and lose some pungent scandal.

"Oh, no!' replied Ezekiel. "They were by far too sweet for that. Eh, My-*rindy?* Did you notice how they seemed to lean and hang on one another?"

"I didn't look at them!" replied Miranda, with a lofty look of scorn.

"What is our duty in the matter?" asked the Austere Member; and she spoke as though she thought they really had a duty in the matter.

"*I* think," said one, "that we should keep an eye on them."

"And so do I," another said: and that opinion seemed to have the support of all.

"Mr. P-e-l-t-e-e-r," suggested another, "why can't you keep watch?"

"I never shrink from duty, ma'am!" was Ezekiel's noble answer; and he secretly rejoiced that he could gratify himself under a commission so high-sounding as that of duty. Before the Board adjourned, Ezekiel was commissioned.

For many days, in spite of all his diligence, Mr. Pelter's watch was unsuccessful. But perseverance, in the end, unless exhausted in attempts at the impossible — a limitation which makes a fallacious adage nearer true — will succeed. He at last espied the "other *woo*-man." She was engaged in shopping on a business street, and after Mr. Pelter had caught sight of her, he gave no opportunity for escape.

Julia, in her pre-occupation, and in the hurrying throng upon the street, did not notice him. Had she been even more observing, she would not have seen him, for he dodged and concealed himself in a way that would have honored a professional detective.

Usually, Julia had her carriage with her, but now it was laid up with some rheumatic difficulty, and she patronized the more democratic carriages of the streets. Ezekiel followed her from place to place, until he felt nearly ready to give up the chase, when he saw her call a stage. He hurried forward and stepped in behind her. Now Julia noticed him, and a smile began to play upon her face. Ezekiel regarded her as another victim, and his sympathetic heart was most decidedly moved in her direction. But, of course, he did not speak to her. At length she stopped the stage.

As she stepped out, Ezekiel followed her. When she reached the pavement and started on, she looked around and saw him following. At this, she stopped before a window, and began to look at articles there displayed for sale, thinking that Ezekiel would pass. But he also stopped before another window, and holding up his eye-glasses, seemed entirely absorbed in something unusually attractive there. Seeing this, Julia started on. Then Ezekiel also started on. She walked faster; and so did he, until he began to sweat and blow. Then she checked her pace, and walked very, very slow; and so did he.

"Now, convinced that he was really after her, she hurried on, her feet winged with fear, until she turned into another street and reached her house. She ran up the steps and rang the bell. Then she turned around to look for her pursuer. There he stood, but a little distance off, looking at a house across the street, as though examining it with a view to purchase.

As soon as she had disappeared within, Ezekiel walked along until he reached the house. He saw a man engaged in shaving the well-kept lawn, and stopped. Resting his arms upon the fence, he looked over.

"A—hem!" said Mr. Pelter. And the man looked up.

Mr. Pelter smiled and said: "Fine grounds, sir."

The man, without replying, turned to his work again.

"A—hem!" said Mr. Pelter, a little louder than before; and the man looked up again.

"Will you step here a moment?" asked Mr. Pelter. The man walked up to him.

"Who lives here?" Ezekiel inquired.

"Mr. Smith."

"Does she live here with him?"

"Who?"

"Why, that woman who just went in."

"Pretty likely, sir, for that's his wife."

"His—wife!" exclaimed Ezekiel. "Two wives on hand, and looking for another! Oh, *what* a world! what a wicked world!" Saying this, he turned and walked away.

"What did that man want?" asked Julia, from a chamber window where she had been standing on the watch.

"Why, ma'am," the man replied, looking up to her, "he's crazy."

"What did he want, I ask!"

"He asked me who lived here."

"Well?"

"I told him Mr. Smith."

"Well!"

"He asked if you lived here."

"Well?"

"I told him yes."

"Well, well—go on!"

"Then he said: 'Two wives on hand, and looking for another!'"

"Is that all?"

"That's all, ma'am."

"What did he mean by that?"

"Don't know, ma'am—he did n't say—that's all he said."

Julia withdrew, and put this conversation in her place for curiosities.

When Mr. Pelter met the Board again he was big with his discovery. His zeal was specially commended, and every one declared that the "work" was progressing favorably.

"Now, if we only had what the lawyers call the *flagrante delicto*, we could take active measures!" one exclaimed.

"Do you suppose," was the judicial inquiry of the Austere Member, speaking to Mr. Pelter, "that you can track the man himself to his adulterous nest?"

"I can try," replied Ezekiel; implying by his tone and manner that he felt quite certain of his ability to do so.

"Then do it," said the Board.

This important matter being settled, and there being nothing further of special interest in the missionary field, the Board adjourned, to meet again when Mr. Pelter should be ready to report.

How little are such guardians of our private virtues appreciated by the vulgar throng!

"But," as Ezekiel says, "their reward is sure to come; in another world, if not in this." Will it smell of brimstone?

Another interval of unsuccessful effort on the part of Mr. Pelter. He gets occasional glimpses of the man he hunts, but he can not track him to his "nest" without discovering himself. This, for obvious reasons, he is anxious to avoid: he has not forgotten his ungraceful exit from Joseph's house. He resolves, at last, to change his plan of operations—to wait for a dark and moonless night, when the unsuspecting man will be snugly housed; unless he is absent with his other wife: in which event another trial must be made.

Under cover of the darkness he could look through illuminated windows, and, unperceived himself, see everything within. It was as dark as Erebus when he set out. He found the place, and paused a moment to consider the most favorable approach. He would be less liable to observation from the street if he selected his position in the rear. This determined him. Very cautiously he made his way around the house. Not a sound was heard, except the muffled palpitations of Ezekiel's heart. Suddenly he stumbled over some unseen object in the dark. With a blessing on his pious lips, he fell upon "all fours," with his bland face in a thorny bush; now up again, he stumbled on his way. At last he saw a flood of light streaming from the windows in the rear; the windows were too high. He walked back toward the stable, to change the angle of his vision, and finally, he could just perceive the heads of John and Julia in the room.

"He's there!" said Mr. Pelter to himself, and he began to feel about, to find some object on which to stand for a better view. He found at last a barrel — one used in carrying coal from the alley to the house. With a word of gratulation, he turned this over,—"bottom up." By great exertion he finally succeeded in getting on and standing up. Now his view was clear and he saw distinctly. What he saw was sufficient to satisfy the Board with exclamations for weeks to come.

He saw Julia rise, and go up to John, and then — sit down: not on another chair, but *on the lap* of the suspected John! Before he had recovered from astonishment at seeing this, his attention was required in a matter more exciting.

The house-dog, having been restrained by the

coachman in the stable, for a few restless moments, now came bounding from the stable door. Ezekiel's odor struck him instantly; and with no reverence for sanctimonious scents, he made a sudden leap, and struck the barrel on which Ezekiel stood. Then ensued an animated conversation; Ezekiel dancing all the time, now on one foot, now on the other, on the barrel-head.

"Good doggie!" said Ezekiel, in his most persuasive tone; and then he jumped, to save his bleeding calf from another bite.

"Bow-wow-wow!" was the dogged answer; and then another snap, and another jump at Ezekiel's legs.

"So, so; good doggie! *nice* doggie!" continued Mr. Pelter.

"Bow-wow-wow!" the dog again replied.

Now the coachman, thoroughly aroused, rushed forth, with a pitchfork in his hand. "S-c-c-c-ick! sick him, Leo! Hold him there!" the coachman cried, running to the battle-field with his fork in rest.

At this most critical emergency the barrel-head gave way, and Ezekiel dropped. The staves now stood around him as a protecting shield to his bleeding legs. The barrel made a snugger fit than Ezekiel was accustomed to, and he could not have got away if he had attempted to, with no one to prevent.

"Thief! thief! thief!" the coachman shouted as loud as he could cry. "At him, Leo! at him!"

The dog, thus stimulated, barked with greater fury than before.

This confusion very soon attracted those in the house, and John came hurrying out, with Julia and the servants following after him.

"What is the matter?" John called out.

"A thief! We've caught him!" shouted back the coachman.

John ran up, but it was too dark to distinguish anything.

A voice from the darkness now cried out: "Don't kill me, for Heaven's sake! I am not fit to die! I always said I was, but it's not so!"

As John approached the barrel, the voice continued, "O, Mr. Smith, don't let them kill me! I'll get down upon my knees to you! I am not a thief!"

"Get your lantern, Thomas," said John, speaking to the coachman, "and throw some light on this dark subject."

The lantern was already lighted, and the coachman went and returned with it within the instant. John took the lantern and held it up to Mr. Pelter's face, and knew it at a glance; then looking at the barrel-trap, he laughed, and shouted: "By all that's wonderful! A barrel-full of charity!"

Ezekiel groaned.

"What are you doing here, and at such a time of night?" asked John, when sufficiently recovered.

"Oh, sir!" said Mr. Pelter from the barrel, "if you will let me off this time, I'll never trouble you again!"

"But what, in the name of mischief, are you here *for?*" persisted John.

"You forget that you are not alone!" replied Ezekiel, speaking in a lower tone, intended for John's private ear. But Julia heard him, and inquired, "What's that?" He did not answer. She was curious.

"Help him out of here," said she, "and bring him to the house for examination."

They contrived to pull him out, and John continued: "Now walk on, and we will follow."

When they reached the house, John conducted Mr. Pelter to the room where he had seen the shocking sight. Here the good man's sad condition was, for the first time, fairly visible. His face was scratched by the thorny bush on which he fell, and some blood had started from the scratches. While engaged with Leo at the barrel, excessive perspiration had flowed the blood to untouched portions of his face; and when he was finally released, he passed his coal-black hands down and across his face, and streaked it with his fingers; so his look was more like a savage, smeared for the war path, than the meek dependent of the Ladies' Board. His spotless waistcoat was all black with coal, and his lower garments were torn and soiled in many places. All this, with Mr. Pelter's frightened looks, was too much for Julia's gravity; and in spite of all the stuffing in her mouth — for she had crammed in her handkerchief — she suddenly exploded with such a ring of laughter as set the servants in a roar, where they were canvassing the situation. John was nearly overcome as well, but he managed to restrain himself, and, smiling, said:

"Now, sir, let us hear what you have to say."

Ezekiel, without speaking, slyly made a motion with his thumb in the direction of the laughing Julia. John could not comprehend this digital expression, and he spoke again — now with some impatience.

"Well, well, go on!"

Had Mr. Pelter been in a less dangerous situation, and free from all embarrassment, he would undoubtedly have improved the present opportunity to rebuke, with great severity, what he regarded as the sinful lives of John and Julia; but prudential thoughts restrained him.

He thought that by concealing what he supposed he knew of John's relation to the jealous

"Mr. Pelter slyly made a motion with his thumb in the direction of the laughing Julia."

Rachel, he would conciliate the dangerous man. So he cautiously replied:

"I was only standing on the barrel, sir, and looking in."

"But what possessed you to come and look in here?" asked Julia; now connecting in her mind this strange behavior with that of Mr. Pelter's following her, and his strange remark as to John's "other *woo*-man," and the dual wives.

"Why, ma'am," Ezekiel answered, with some confusion, "I wanted—to see—if you were here together—that's all."

This answer only deepened the mystery; and Julia was about to continue her examination, when John turned to her and said:

"I believe the man is cracked. At all events, there seems to be no sense in what he says. I think we had better let him off; he has been severely punished, as it is, for his foolish curiosity."

"Oh, yes!—by all means!—let him go!—if you wish it so."

Her suspicions were thoroughly aroused by what seemed to her John's anxiety to get Ezekiel off.

"Then you may go," said John; "and let this experience be a lesson to you."

Ezekiel was not long in going; and when he found himself alone, he said: "It was a lucky thing for me that I knew about his Rachel! That knowledge saved me. It would not *do* to be severe with me. *I might tell!* But what will Mrs. Pelter say when she sees me in this condition? She 'll put me *in* the wash-tub now, I fear."

His duty first was to report to Rachel; and even in his soiled and tattered garments he made his way to Rachel's house, and there reported his discovery. With serious misgivings, he now proceeded to confront his "cross." What Mrs. Pelter really did, or what she said to him, was never known. He would never speak of it. But it was remarked, after that unlucky night, that he stood in greater fear of his spirited companion than before; and it was also noticed that, after that, when she cried "PELTER!" he bounded like a rubber ball. His face, too, had a careworn look, which all his blandness could not entirely conceal.

After Mr. Pelter left the house, John and Julia began to discuss the matter.

"This looks very strange to me," said Julia. "Why should that man take such pains to look in here?"

"I do n't know," was John's reply; "but as near as I can ascertain, he belongs to a board of meddlers in other people's matters."

"But why should such a Board direct its inquiries in this direction? What is there here to excite their curiosity? That's what puzzles me!"

"Well, I admit it's strange; and I don't understand it any better than yourself."

"Why did you dismiss him before he was thoroughly examined?"

"I spoke to you before dismissing him, and I understood you to assent to it."

"I assented, because you proposed it."

"Did you wish to question him?"

"Well—yes. I did."

"You should have said so, then."

"You seemed in such a hurry to get him off.

"In a hurry! Why no, my dear; except that I did not care to hear his foolish talk."

John spoke so naturally, and with such a show of perfect frankness, that Julia began to question her suspicions. Then she thought that she would see if John, in any way, could clear up some other doubts.

"Do you know," said she, "that this same Pelter followed me all the way from down town the other day?"

"No," John answered. "But was he following you? Was he not by chance going in the same direction?"

"He was following me! I tested him sufficiently to know. Besides, after I came in, he stopped and questioned Thomas. He asked who lived here, and when Thomas told him, he asked if I lived here with you. Thomas told him that I did, and that I was your wife. What do you suppose he said?"

"That I was a lucky fellow."

"He said, 'two wives on hand, and looking for another!' What did he mean by that?"

"Why the man is crazy! I more than half thought so before, but now it's clear. What man in his senses would get off such twaddle? When I met him first he acted in a very curious way, and I thought that he was drunk—but that I told you of."

"Then, when he met us on the street, and spoke of your 'other *woo*-man,' he was crazy too?"

"No doubt of it. I can understand it now. He has something on his crazy mind about a woman, and, perhaps, when he saw us on the street that day, he associated you with her. Queer freaks these fellows have sometimes. This also will account for his following you, and for his appearance here to-night. No sane man would have perched himself upon a barrel, in the back yard, to see if we were in, when a thousand simpler ways were open to him. He could have rung the bell, and walked *in* to see us. It must be that the fellow's daft. I'm glad that we were easy on him."

All this seemed possible, and even reasonable, Julia thought. And she was satisfied.

For some days after this Mr. Pelter did not leave his house. These were dark days: and even to *this* day a veil of darkness hides them. But in these dark days the scratches on Ezekiel's face and the bites upon his legs were healed. Then Ezekiel emerged. And there was nothing in his dress or look to recall the unlucky night. But in Mr. Pelter's manner there was something strange. He never stopped upon the street without looking around, as though upon the watch; and sometimes he would fancy that he saw the object of his fear, and then he would dodge and conceal himself, or turn quickly into another street. This fear was ever-present with him, and he could not shake it off, for it dogged him — everywhere. A future chapter will disclose the nature of this fear.

After he emerged, he sent notice to the Board, and named a day when he would meet them at their rooms. At the appointed time, they all assembled there, and when Mr. Pelter entered he was greeted and much comforted by their applause. It was understood among them that he had made some astonishing discoveries, and that the "cause" was much indebted to his moral courage. They were impatient for the details. Mr. Pelter's natural modesty inclined him to attempt to check the enthusiasm of the Board in his behalf; but somehow, as it always happened in such attempts, his words and manner only served to make himself more prominent.

"It is not myself," said he, on this occasion, "but the cause of virtue that has triumphed! *I* am but a worm! an humble instrument!"

This was very modest in Ezekiel, but any one could see by his self-satisfied expression that he *did* take personal credit, and feel a personal triumph, and that he believed that all the virtues revolved around himself and made their center there. It was noticed, as he spoke, that withal there was an anxious look upon his face, and the cause of this he now proceeded to explain.

"I am walking in the constant fear of death!" said he. "At any moment I may be stricken down by this bold adulterer—this man of sin! If I fall, let it be remembered of me that I fell in the noble cause of duty!"

It is impossible to describe the imposing attitude of Mr. Pelter as he delivered these affecting words. The effect upon the Board was most profound.

"In the cause of duty," continued Mr. Pelter, "I am fearless! Let the base assassin strike! he will strike a fearless heart!"

"What a noble man!" said a weeping member.

"He shall not strike you," sobbed Miranda.

"But, to my report," continued Mr. Pelter, and all were curious. "Our worst suspicions are confirmed! I have visited the abode of sin, and I saw the damning proof! It is for this he threatens me, and seeks my life!"

The sensation here was equal to Ezekiel's wishes, and he paused to give it full effect.

"I saw," said he, impressively, and with great deliberation, that handsome *woo*-man—sit down—" Here he stopped abruptly and looked at his "Mi-*rindy*."

"Go on! Go on!" cried out the excited members.

"Shall I go on?" said he, with his eyes still fixed on the gushing vessel, "and blush those virgin cheeks with shame?"

"Oh, do go on!" called out the vessel, not blushing in the least.

"I saw her — sit down," resumed Ezekiel, "upon — his — l-a-p!"

"Oh, shame!" "Shame!" "Shame!" cried the members of the Board; and Miranda now put up her hands as if to hide her blushes — although, in fact, there were no blushes there to hide.

"But how was it, Mr. P-e-l-t-e-e-r," a member asked, "that you saw all this? Did you go in?"

"I did," replied Ezekiel: but from some

strange forgetfulness at the instant, or from the excitement of the occasion, he did not make the most distant reference to his point of observation, or to the manner of his entry. He then related how, on the following day, Joseph Smith came in search of him, and when he could not find him, how he frightened Mrs. Pelter by his murderous threats. In all of this, Ezekiel made himself appear to be a much braver man than he really was, and he assigned a cause for Joseph's anger quite different from the actual cause, as will appear when the proper scene is introduced. This is to be regretted, since many readers may be inclined to question Ezekiel's veracity, rather than to admire his peculiar imagery. He was never known to swerve from the truth, when the truth would serve as well as imagery.

The Board now centered all its sympathy on the forsaken Rachel.

CHAPTER VI.

TABLEAUX VIVANTS.

WHEN Rachel left the ladies' rooms, with Joseph following her, she made every effort to avoid him, but unsuccessfully. He followed her with prayers and protestations, and would not be shaken off; but she did not reply to him by so much as a single word. Thus they walked along until they reached their carriage. Then she turned to him, and said:

"Which one of us shall get in here?"

"Yourself, of course, if only one," he answered.

She stepped in, and he stood still until the carriage turned and drove away.

The whole affair was so incomprehensible to him that he knew not what to do. He saw that in Rachel's present state he could not talk with her, and who else could furnish him a clue? Could it be possible that he had visited the Board without knowing it himself? This could not be possible, of course, unless his mind had been aberrant. Had it been? The positive assertions of all the members, and of Miranda Trap, certainly seemed to show that he had been there. Was his mind in any way disordered, and yet he, apparently, in the full possession of his faculties?

"No madman was ever yet convinced of his own insanity," he thought; "and if my mind is touched, that would account for everything." But such reflections were too absurd, and he abruptly broke them off.

When he first concluded to settle in New York, he invested nearly all his funds in a manufacturing establishment in New Jersey, and in some vessels engaged in trade and transportation to foreign countries.

The factory in New Jersey was in a quiet, pleasant spot, and Joseph made occasional visits there, remaining sometimes for several days together. Now he thought of this quiet spot, as a place of rest from his distractions, until his wife should find a better and more temperate mind. He no longer thought of insisting upon an explanation of Mr. Pelter's questionable appearance in his house, for if Rachel should deign to answer him at all, she would answer by a counter-charge, no doubt. It would be best, he thought, for many reasons, to leave passion time to cool, and to avoid all further conflicts for the present.

So he determined to make a visit to the factory; and with this determination he started for his house.

"Rachel," said he, when he saw his wife, "I have concluded to make a visit to the factory, and let our troubles rest until our minds are settled, and we can talk them over calmly."

Rachel was too strong a woman to be easily crushed by troubles, but she could petrify; and so she turned to stone.

"My mind is settled now!" she answered. "If you need sedatives, take them in any form you please. It will occupy some time, I think, for you to arrange a plausible theory of defense; take your time — and make it strong. I shall manage to exist if you are absent for awhile."

"I see that it is useless to attempt to talk at present," responded Joseph.

"Entirely useless!" was the answer. "I have lost faith in you! Do you know what that means? Do you know what it is to lose another's confidence?"

"Well, well; no matter now. I shall not be absent very long, and hope to find you in a better mind when I come back."

She did not answer this; and Joseph went out to pack up his things. Very soon he left the house.

Nothing could have suited Rachel better than

Joseph's absence for awhile. She could now take any measures deemed expedient for securing proofs of Joseph's guilt, and without the fear of interruption. She soon stated her intentions to the Ladies' Board, and found in them a corps of ready helpers. They advised her to confide in Mr. Pelter, and be governed by his knowledge and experience. This advice was agreeable to her.

There is a subtile law, pertaining to the action of our hearts, which resembles that so often quoted by physical philosophers as a general law of nature — it abhors a vacuum.

This abhorrence was in Rachel's nature, as well as in that of gentler women; and she could not help contrasting Mr. Pelter, on his knees, suffering from a vacuum, and Joseph with his vacuum doubly filled. Wintry smiles began to flit across her stony face, and sometimes even warmer ones. But they found the place so strange, at first, that they did not linger there. That they came at all was evidence that Rachel had begun to modify the rigid maxims of her life. Mr. Pelter must have been a man of wondrous power, to make a change so marvelous.

The ladies told her where Ezekiel lived; and a few days after Joseph left she resolved to call upon him. Mrs. Pelter saw her when she left her carriage at the gate, and started for the door;

and so did Mr. Pelter. Both thought to meet her at the door, and both started — but Ezekiel was first.

His wife retired with a frown upon her face, and he received the visitor. He showed her to his little room, and she at once commenced:

"I have come to ask your help again."

"I am always at your service, madam," replied Ezekiel, with a bow.

The wintry smiles began to flicker feebly on Rachel's face again, as she responded:

"You are very kind."

"What is it now?" asked Mr. Pelter, in a business way.

"It is — trouble! Mr. P-e-l-t-e-e-r;" and Rachel struck the lingering accent on his name.

Mr. Pelter's gentle heart was touched, and so profoundly touched that even his My-*rindy* was forgotten. There was a look of more than sympathy in his inquiring eyes, but Rachel did not notice it.

"Trouble?" he repeated. "And have you heard of it?"

"Of what?" she asked.

"Did you not tell the ladies that your husband was at the factory, in New Jersey?"

"Yes."

"And do you still believe that he is there?"

"Yes."

"Then you have *not* heard of it!"

"Of what?"

"Of your husband's latest!"

"Latest what?"

"Latest WOO-MAN!"

"Another one?"

"Another!"

Rachel's fortitude was tried at last, and she began to break.

"Tell me," was all that she could utter.

"He is not at the factory! He is in the city!"

"Go on!"

"I saw him yesterday!"

"Ah! now I see you are mistaken. If he had been here yesterday, I should have seen him — he would have been at home."

"He should have been at home."

"He *would* have been, I say!"

"But he was not!"

"He was not in the city!"

"I saw him!"

"It was a mistake!"

"My-*rindy* saw him!"

"She was mistaken!"

"We met him face to face — and he spoke to us — with the *woo*-man hanging on his arm!"

"This, then," said Rachel, with a sudden flash of rage, "is the secret of his frequent visits to the factory! O, what a shocking factory! Who is she? Can you tell me who she is, and where she can be found?"

"Not yet," said Mr. Pelter, "but I shall track her to the nest, and then I'll tell you."

For a moment Rachel's look was one of stupefaction and absolute despair. She began to grope as if in darkness, and to totter as if about to fall. Mr. Pelter, seeing this, stretched out his arms to catch her, and called out:

"Rachel!"

At this very instant, Mrs. Pelter's head popped through the door, and she cried:

"PELTER!" and then popped back again.

Rachel did not fall, nor did Mr. Pelter touch her, but she put one hand upon her forehead, and stood a moment speechless; then the long-sealed fountain of her tears gave way, and she sobbed as though her heart was broken.

This was no time for sentimental thoughts or speech, on the part of Mr. Pelter, for there was a passion quivering in his presence which dwarfed and stunned him.

"God help me!" was all she said, when, by great effort, she had sufficiently recovered; and, with tears upon her cheeks, she turned and left the house.

Rachel's agony had a human termination. After she had reached her home and reflected on this new development, all her other passions were subjected to the ruling one of hate. She resolved to find the woman who hung on Joseph's arm — for she *hated* her.

After Mr. Pelter had followed Julia home and made his inquiries of Thomas, as recorded in a previous chapter, he hastened to report the facts to Rachel. She would have gone at once and confronted Julia, but Ezekiel advised her to be patient, and wait until he had caught Joseph there, and made the case too clear for contradiction.

On that unlucky night when, from his position on the barrel-head, Mr. Pelter saw the shocking sight, Rachel was startled by a visit from the begrimed and battered man.

"They 're caught!" said he.

And then he told his story; and she could see how much he had suffered in her service. Promising to meet again they parted, for it was late, and Ezekiel must hasten home.

The proof of Joseph's infidelity was now regarded as complete; and Rachel was impatient for the day of his arraignment.

Joseph remained longer in New Jersey than he had intended when he left his house; and when he reached New York again, he was advised that a vessel in which he was part owner was ready for another voyage — indeed it had been ready for several hours, and was only waiting for his return. It was nearly night when he arrived, and without delay he went on board to inspect the cargo, and give some final orders and instructions. He was detained for several hours, and until late at night; so late, that he resolved to "turn in" there for the remainder of the night. This was the unlucky night of Ezekiel's visit to the house of John, when he saw the shocking sight. On the following morning, early, he went ashore, and the vessel sailed.

Now he started for his house, and on the way was occupied by his perplexities: he little dreamed how much they had been complicated since he left his house. He soon found Rachel, and in a glad and hopeful voice saluted her; attempting even a caress more affectionate than usual.

She drew away from him with a look of absolute disgust.

"Why, Rachel," said he, in astonishment, "is this your greeting?"

She did not even answer him, and walked away.

"We must arrive at some understanding in this matter," said Joseph to himself. "I can not live in this way!" And with a look of some determination, he started after Rachel. He found her seated in another room.

"Rachel," said he, "if you will help me in this matter, we can probably arrive at some satisfactory solution. I have tried without your help, and only grope in darkness. This Miranda Trap is like the Old Man of the Sea to me; and unless I shake her off, she'll ride me to distraction. There *is* an explanation, if we can only find it."

"Your affair with Miranda Trap," said Rachel, in an icy tone, "was fortunately discovered in time to save her."

"I tell you," said Joseph, with impatience, "that I never had an affair with Miranda Trap!"

"So you said before," said Rachel, in a tone most aggravating.

"Rachel!" retorted Joseph, angrily, "you seem to have forgotten what I saw in this very room! and that there is an explanation due to me. Are you attempting to cover it by these ridiculous and baseless charges? Remember that it was not a shadow that *I* saw."

"Sir!" said Rachel, flaming instantly, and rising to her feet, "there are other charges, and very far from shadowy ones, which you must meet! You will find them much more serious and perplexing than what you call the 'ridiculous and baseless ones.' They, at least, are supported by the most substantial proof!"

"Other charges!" repeated Joseph, with a

sneer. "What other charges? Name them! All! And let's have done with nonsense. I am tired of this everlasting mystery and innuendo. If you will not have peace!—and insist on war!—unmask your batteries! I am disgusted with this trifling!"

Rachel saw a storm in Joseph's face; but she felt too well armed to tremble, and she answered promptly:

"Another of your amours has been brought to light!"

"For heaven's sake, speak out! I tell you that I am tired of insinuations! Name your charges!"

"Very well." Here Rachel's face was white. "I charge you with pretending to be absent in New Jersey, when, in fact, you are in the city here with a handsome and voluptuous woman! I ——"

"Go on! go on! Let's see how far your foolish jealousy will lead you!"

"You have been seen with this handsome and voluptuous woman upon your lap! And I know the very house where you live in shameless adultery together! Are the charges clear—and free from 'mystery'—and '*innuendo*'—and 'insinuation'?"

"They are monstrous lies! and so *monstrous* in their character as to make me doubt your sanity!"

"I have the proof! the *proof!!* the PROOF!!!" now cried Rachel, furious with passion.

"You — have — no — such — thing!" answered Joseph, so terribly in earnest that he was white and calm. "But *I* have proof—and can produce it — to show that I have *not* been in the city since I left you here!"

"Where were you last night?" asked Rachel. "In New Jersey?"

"Last night I was detained by business until nearly morning ——"

"Ha! ha! ha! Not in New Jersey, though?"

"No."

"I know it! and I know what your '*business*' was. You were caught last night! You thought that Mr. Pelter would not tell!"

"Mr. Pelter! — would not tell? Why, woman, I was on board a vessel!"

"Perhaps you have proof of *that?*"

"The vessel sailed this morning, and of course I have not the proof at present, but when she returns I can furnish proof."

"This, then, is the way you have arranged to meet the charge, if Mr. Pelter should report! What a convenient thing that vessel was! Of course she carried off your proof! Now, sir, it must be evident to you that you have been exposed! I could even send you to the penitentiary as a bigâmist!"

"You have gone too far to stop at this," said Joseph, now *very* calm. "These charges are too serious to be trifled with. Explain yourself!"

"I shall tell you nothing more," said Rachel. "You know it all! You would like to ascertain, no doubt, how much I know, that you may trim your sails accordingly. You may rest assured that I know enough—too much, indeed! What I may conclude to do, is yet an open question. You will learn in proper time."

With this she turned from him again, and again went out and left him.

"That rascally Pelter has been here," said Joseph to himself. "He is the author of this mischief, and he shall explain it to me. I'll go to him at once!"

Then he started from the house. He was not long in finding where Mr. Pelter lived, and soon found the house. But Mr. Pelter was laid up with the injuries received the night before in the grounds of John; and Mrs. Pelter so far observed his wishes as to say to all that he was not able to see visitors.

"Is Mr. Pelter in?" asked Joseph, when she had answered to his ring.

"He is in his room, sir; but at present he is not able to see visitors," was her reply. "I will take your name and give it to him, and he will see you when he is able."

"My name is Smith," said Joseph; "but no matter; I will call again."

"Are you *Joseph* Smith?" asked Mrs. Pelter, with a sudden interest.

"Yes," he answered.

"Come in! come in, sir! I want to talk with you," insisted she. He stepped in and followed her.

Ezekiel, in his little room, had heard the bell, and when he heard the sound of voices at the door, he was curious. As he approached *his* door he heard his wife invite the visitor to enter; and now he was more curious than before. As soon as they had passed his door he opened it a little way and peeped out. He saw and recognized the visitor at once. Feeling a sudden weakness in his knees, he softly closed the door and took out his large and spotless handkerchief, and wiped his face.

"He is after me!" said he; and then he softly locked the door, and drew his table up against it, and sat down on the table. He waited thus, with palpitating heart, for some little time; and when Joseph did not come out, he began to think that he had another object in his visit.

"Is he after Mrs. Pelter for his harem?" was his mental question; and when he thought it possible, he gave soft expression to his horror. "O, *what* a world! What a *wicked* world!" said he.

When Mrs. Pelter and the visitor were seated, she said to him:

"Since your wife and my husband have commenced to intrigue, I think it best for us to join against them."

"Do you charge my wife with an improper intrigue?" asked Joseph, with a frown.

"Well — yes. That's what *I* call it. I believe the ladies of the Board have some other name for it — they give very pious names sometimes to what seems irregular, at least to me." Saying this, she excused herself, and went into another room, leaving Joseph on tenter-hooks. She soon returned with a letter in her hand.

"You know your wife's handwriting, I suppose?" said she, in a bustling, business way, but with a revengeful sparkle in her eyes.

"Of course I do."

"Read that!" and here she handed him the letter she had taken from Ezekiel's coat.

He took and read it carefully and without a word. But there was a fearful change in the expression of his face. When he spoke again he was very calm — too calm; and Mrs. Pelter saw a wicked passion in his eyes.

"Where did you get this letter?" he inquired.

"I found it in my husband's pocket."

"You must let me have it."

"You can have it, sir; I have no further use for it."

"I HAVE!" said he; and he spoke in such a tone as frightened her. "Your husband," he continued, "went there, I suppose — went to see my wife — his 'lamb,' as she calls herself?"

"Oh yes, sir."

"And they have met each other since?"

"Oh yes."

"At my house?"

"She came here to see him once."

"Indeed! What passed between them here?"

"You can judge, perhaps, when I tell you what I saw."

"What did you see?"

"They were in Mr. Pelter's little room together, and I went up softly and opened the door, and put in my head ——"

"Well?"

"Well; he said, 'Rachel!' and with open arms stepped up, when I cried 'PELTER!' and frightened them."

"Well?"

"That 's all, sir; I backed out again."

"Woman!" said Joseph, starting up, "do you know what you are saying?"

"Why how you look," she answered; "you 're enough to frighten one! Of course I know what I am saying."

"Do you care much for your husband?"

"Do I *care* for him?"

"Yes. Would you care much if something happened to him?"

"How?"

"If he should get hurt!"

"O, sir! now I understand you. Of course I care for him — too much to have him hurt! He 's spooney, sometimes, but after all he 's my husband."

"Then keep him from my path! I will not look for him — on your account — but let him keep away from me, or he will get hurt?"

"O, what have I done?" cried Mrs. Pelter, in alarm. "You must promise me —"

Before she could finish what she was about to say, Joseph was rushing from the house on his way home again. No sooner was he out of sight than Mrs. Pelter hurried to Ezekiel, and soon frightened him more thoroughly than *she* was frightened.

"Do you know who was here just now?" she asked.

"Yes," he answered, "it was Joseph Smith."

"And you are a lucky man to have escaped him!"

"How?" asked Mr. Pelter, trembling. "What — did — he — w-a-n-t?"

"He wanted you!"

"Oh, dear! Oh, dear! what does he want of me?"

"He wants to punish you! He wants to kill you!"

Ezekiel groaned. His legs shook so that he could scarcely stand.

"Oh, wife!" said he, as he settled down into a chair, and turned his white, scared face on Mrs. Pelter, "if the Lord will only save me this time I'll be a better man! Indeed — indeed — I will!"

"Keep away from Joseph Smith, and save yourself," said she. "The Lord don't manage our private matters; He is in better business!"

This was the fear which, after that, haunted Mr. Pelter whenever he walked abroad; and for which he gave a different cause, in speaking to the ladies of the Board.

When Joseph reached his house again, and Rachel saw him, she knew that there was some desperate purpose in his mind. She could see it in every look and motion, and before he spoke a word. In spite of every effort at composure, she trembled as she met him.

"I have the 'key,'" said he. "You said the 'key' would explain it all, and make it clear — and *so it does!*"

"What — do — you — mean?" she asked, in a low, scared voice.

"When, in my perplexity and distraction, I

asked you that question, you refused to answer me. *I* will *not* refuse to answer. Shame on you! Shame! Shame! Shame! Now I see why you trumped up charges to worry me! It was to cover your short-comings! Look at that!"

Here he threw down the letter he had received from Mrs. Pelter, and spurned it with his foot.

Rachel was so overpowered by astonishment that she could not move.

"Look at it, I say!" continued he.

She stooped and picked up the letter, and recognized it. She turned from white to red, and from red to white.

"You are Mr. Pelter's 'lamb,' are you?" he commenced again.

"Oh!" she quickly cried, "that did not refer to me! It referred to Miranda Trap!"

"Have done with Miranda Trap!" he thundered. "You have played upon that string as long as it will sound for you! Hear *me* play on it now, and see if you enjoy the sound as much as *I* did! Was it Miranda Trap who wrote to Mr. Pelter to come to her when her husband was away, and they would be undisturbed? Was it Miranda Trap before whom the sanctimonious lubber kneeled, in this very room? Was it Miranda Trap who even went to visit him, and who was discovered in his room with him, and whom he called 'Rachel!' as he stretched out his arms for an embrace? Oh, it was an oversight in you to refuse to talk with me, and to send me hunting for an explanation of my difficulties!"

Rachel, with wild and staring eyes, stood rooted to the spot. She could not speak; she tried to, but was paralyzed. The letter by itself she might explain, but the scene in Mr. Pelter's room she could not explain to the satisfaction of a jealous and suspicious mind. It would support the worst constructions of the language of the letter. After struggling for a time, while he intently watched her, she found a voice to speak. It was a strange, unnatural voice, and full of agony.

"Oh, Joseph, strike me if you will! Kill me if you will! I am not as guilty as you think me, but yet I am not free from guilt! I should have been more frank with you. Do what you please; say what you please! In the present temper of our minds I cannot explain! This much I'll say — and God knows I speak the truth — I am better, far better, than you think me; though not so good as I profess to be!"

Her evident distress touched Joseph's magnanimity, and he replied:

"Let us drop the subject for the present."

Rachel was quick to accept the proffered truce,

and for the time the warfare was suspended. Then Joseph left the house again to go where business duties called him.

Rachel's reflections were very bitter. In spite of his supposed misconduct, and what she regarded as the conclusive proof of it, he held her at advantage by his discovery of her imprudence. Mr. Pelter was the only witness as to Joseph's infidelity, and now he would be discredited and made to appear a dishonorable conspirator. Joseph still denied his guilt, and could continue to successfully deny it, unless the proof was stronger.

"If *I* could only catch them! And I will if such a thing is possible," she said.

To accomplish this, it would be necessary to communicate again with Mr. Pelter; for he was the only one who knew and could identify the woman. As she thought of this, she felt inclined at first to abandon the attempt; for if Joseph should discover another private meeting with Mr. Pelter, her case would be a desperate one. "But," she reflected, "it is desperate now, and I must take the risk."

She could not go again to Mr. Pelter's house, and she did not dare to write to him; but she could arrange to meet him at the ladies' rooms, and this, at length, she determined on.

CHAPTER VII.

JOSEPH WRESTLES WITH TEMPTATION.

RACHEL would not be precipitate. Joseph might admit his guilt, and render further *espionage* unnecessary.

But, as days passed by, he did not confess, nor in any way refer to the charges made. Evidently he expected her to speak, and when she continued silent, he grew colder and more distant. She *would* not speak until she could confound him by her personal observations. She felt quite certain of finding him with the suspected woman before very long, for she concluded that he must manage somehow to divide his time between them; and she thought when he told one that he was at the factory, he was really with the other.

So matters rested until Ezekiel's scratches healed, and he had made his astonishing report to the ladies' Board.

Shortly after this, Rachel, through the ladies of the Board, arranged to meet Ezekiel at the ladies' rooms. When they met, she urged him to continue his investigations. Up to this time, as has been already shown, the call of duty was to Mr. Pelter like a bugle-call to battle in a veteran army; but now the call was drowned in the louder cry of fear, and he was not so ready as before to confront the wrath of Joseph, even with his Christian armor on. But after much persuasion, he finally consented; for in spite of all his fears, he had great confidence in his dodging capabilities. It was arranged that on the following day, at a certain hour, Rachel should meet him on Broadway in a hired carriage. The place agreed upon was near where Ezekiel had previously encountered Julia, when she was engaged in shopping. And the carriage was to be a hired one, that it might be less likely to attract attention than her own if Joseph should appear. It was thought to be quite likely that Julia would be found again engaged in shopping there; and if she was not, then they could drive to the neighborhood where Julia lived, and arrange for observations from that locality.

On the following day, as the appointed hour drew near, the Fates seemed all propitious. Ezekiel, in his impatience, arrived in advance of the hour named; and it was fortunate that it so happened. He had hardly reached the place, when he saw Joseph coming from the opposite direction. He dodged and skipped with great agility, until he had crossed the street; then he very quickly turned around and saw Joseph enter a shop opposite, where gentlemen's clothing was kept for sale. He did not come out immediately, and while Ezekiel watched the door Rachel drove up in her hired carriage.

Mr. Pelter, now protected by the intervening carriage, hurried back across the street, and from the street-side of the carriage gave Rachel warning of Joseph's presence. With a sudden start, and quivering from excitement, she let fall the carriage curtain, and invited Mr. Pelter to a seat beside her. He lost no time in taking it. Looking from a little peep-hole, which they very soon arranged, at the side of the carriage curtain, they watched the door for Joseph's re-appearance.

He soon came out, dressed *cap-a-pie* in a new and becoming suit of clothes; even his hat was new. They were so engaged in seeing this that they did not notice that at the very moment another carriage came, and stopped immediately in front of them, and very near; nor did they notice that a comely and smiling woman called out from the other carriage, and made Joseph look that way. They saw Joseph turn and stop. Then they looked to see what had stopped him. Their carriage front was slightly turned toward the street, and the other carriage was squarely at the curb-stone, and could be seen from the little peep-hole.

The other carriage was a handsome one and arranged in open style; and they saw a lady in it, beckoning to Joseph. Rachel's eyes were wide with wonder as she took in the sight, and called Ezekiel's attention to it.

"Bless me!" he cried, with a sudden start. "It is — the— v-e-r-y — *woo*-man!"

They could hear her as she spoke to Joseph.

"Come! Get in and go with me!" said she. "I will bring you back after luncheon, if you wish it. I want to talk with you a moment."

Joseph hesitated, and even seemed to be protesting. But she would not listen to him, and at last he did get in, and the handsome carriage turned and drove away.

Rachel, with a white, stern face and compressed lips, called sharply to the driver and ordered him to drive after them. And so he did.

"I want you to go and lunch with me today," said Julia, as she and Joseph drove away. Then, looking in his face, she added: "Why, you look as solemn as a funeral! Somehow — though how I cannot say exactly — but *somehow*, you look almost strange to me. Perhaps it 's that new suit of clothes and a different hat."

Joseph was too full of speculations and growing curiosity to reply at once. "She must know me well," he thought, "to notice that I have another suit of clothes and a different hat."

Julia kept her smiling eyes upon him, and he began to feel the fascinating spell; perhaps he made no effort to resist it. The contrast, certainly, between this face and Rachel's was most striking, and Joseph now was suffering from a vacuum.

But why did she call him? What did she want? At first he thought that she had some business inquiries to make, and that being on the street, and in her carriage, it was natural to call him there. But when she talked simply of taking him to luncheon, and spoke not a word of business, he was puzzled and uneasy. What if he had been entrapped by a charmer of the *demi-monde?* Inwardly he thanked his lucky stars that Rachel could not get hold of this.

"Why do n't you answer me?" Julia asked. "You look worried! What troubles you?"

"Oh," said Joseph, reminded by the question of his domestic troubles, "the very mischief seems to be in everything! I almost wish that I was dead!"

"Cheer up!" said Julia. "In this sad mood you are not like yourself. Even your voice sounds strange. Tell me what troubles you, and it will be curious if we do not make the troubles fly!"

With this, she put her little hand on his—caressingly—and gave him such a tender smile as made him glow, in spite of all his stoicism. In all of his experience he had never been so tempted as at the present moment. Prudence admonished him to stop, and to leave this dangerous enchantress. Then Temptation had a score of ready answers, and even ridiculed his fears.

"Have you not sufficient strength," Temptation said, "to keep yourself from harm? What is the value of your virtuous maxims if they can not support you in an affair so trivial? If she goes too far, then stop; but do not be frightened in advance."

All this had a sound of reason; and if Joseph saw no sophistry, let it be remembered that there was a spell upon him.

If objectors would sit in judgment on him, let them first surround the judgment-seat with such witching eyes as Julia had. It was a happy thought to put a bandage on the eyes of Justice.

Then came other stumbling-blocks in Joseph's way to trip up his virtuous feet. Rachel had destroyed the comforts of his home, and fairly driven him to seek agreeable society abroad; if he found agreeable society, why should he not enjoy it, so long as he did not go too far? He would *not* go too far!

But he had already gone too far; when he *argued* with temptation, he was *then* undone. He should have said, "Behind me!"

When Julia touched his hand, and gave him such a smile, he made no attempt to hold back the sudden tide of pleasure which gulped him in its amorous flood. It was the old, old story. He did not stop to think that turtle-doves, like other birds, are poisoned by the exhalations from the waters of Avernus.

Seeing that Joseph did not seem inclined to tell her of his troubles now, Julia resolved to wait until they could sit down at home, and have sufficient time for a full discussion. She wondered what the trouble was a hundred times, but she did not ask again.

At length she said, thinking to turn the current of his thoughts:

"I had an object in bringing you with me to-day; and it is a selfish one—as usual, perhaps."

"Now," thought Joseph, "she is coming to her business, after all. I shall be glad to know what I am about, for I began to fear that she would muddle me as much as Rachel did."

"I want you," continued she, "to get some tickets for the theater to-night; if we wait till evening the best seats will be taken; you can get them after lunch. Several of my friends are going, and I told them that I would go."

Joseph was shocked. He was one of those who profess to think that theaters are but the gilded gateways to perdition; and it was not strange that he experienced a virtuous recoil as he listened to this proposition, and thought of being seen in such a place with this strange and handsome woman. "What would the brethren and the sisters say? And what would Rachel say?" In truth, with him, as with very many others of like pretensions, the thought of what might be said had greater force by far than the restraints of conscience; but it contributed to his self-righteousness to put it on his conscience, and so he did.

"Impossible!" he answered. "Impossible! I could not think of such a thing!"

Julia's rosy lips were made for pouts as well as smiles, and she pouted now most decidedly.

"Very well, sir,—very well!" she answered, in a pet.

After this, the silence was unbroken until they reached the house. Joseph at once observed that the house was in a respectable, and even fashionable, locality. Before reaching it he had determined that he would not go in, but when he saw the stamp of respectability on its front, he thought that he would not be compromised if he did go in. He did go in. He followed Julia like one walking in a sleep, until she reached her *boudoir;* here she turned to him and said:

"Forget my pet, and forgive me, dear, while I go in and change my dress. No matter about the theater; I should have thought of your annoyances."

Before Joseph could recover from his indescribable astonishment, she retreated, looking back and smiling as she went — to a sleeping-room and closed the door. Joseph felt the power of her charms, and feared if she returned to the assault that he could not resist it. Besides, if she was what she *ought* to be, how could she address him as she did, and receive him — a stranger — in her *boudoir?*

It will be remembered, that in his early days — and before he went to sea — he had resolved that in such a situation he would prove his strength. Here was the first occasion ever offered for the actual test.

"She is another Mrs. Potiphar!" said Joseph to himself, "and I will fly!"

He sat down carefully, and drew off his boots; with these in hand he rose, and with noiseless steps, approached the door. Very softly he unlatched the door and opened it; and then, on noiseless toes, he stole cautiously away. In the vestibule below he pulled on his boots, and then made boldly for the outer door.

A servant saw him as he tip-toed through the hall, with his boots in hand, and she informed

"She retreated, looking back, and smiling as she went to a sleeping room."

another servant, and both hastened to a window to see what he was about.

Julia, hearing the sound of carriage wheels directly after, hurried to her window.

Rachel did not once lose sight of Julia's carriage until it drew up at Julia's door, and had left its occupants and driven off. While Julia and Joseph were getting out and walking up the steps, Rachel stopped. When she saw them enter she started on, and drove slowly past the house and fixed it in her mind. After she had passed a little distance, she had her carriage turn to the most favorable position, and then she stopped to watch.

It was growing very warm for Mr. Pelter now, and he began to perspire freely; the prospect of confronting Joseph was too much for him, and his courage began to ooze away. Rachel was so entirely absorbed in other things that she did not observe his perturbation. Her face had never been so hard as now, nor her look so keen; but there was no other object for that look so keen than Julia's door.

Mr. Pelter grew more restless and excited with every passing moment; and when it seemed that Joseph might appear, before he could escape, his fear found tongue. He entreated Rachel to release him while he had a chance for safety; and had she looked around, she would have been astonished at that frightened face on one who had claimed to be so valiant.

With her eyes on Julia's door, and without moving from her fixed position, she answered in a strange, unnatural tone: "Go!"

With a sigh of infinite relief, the good man wiped his face again, and prepared to go. As he rose up and put his foot upon the carriage step, he looked back across his shoulder, and quickly asked:

"Will you come to the ladies' rooms?"

She did not answer—she did not seem to hear him—and her eyes were fixed on Julia's door.

So Mr. Pelter left her. He hurried to the pavement on the other side from Julia's house, and had almost reached a point directly opposite, when he saw the hall door open and Joseph Smith step out. At the very instant, he heard the crack of the driver's whip and the sound of rapid carriage wheels behind. He looked behind, and saw Rachel's carriage dashing up. He looked across, and saw Joseph watching him as he came down the steps. With terror in his face, and a sudden bound, he ran, with Fear upon his flying heels. As he ran, he turned his head at nearly every step to see if he was pursued. So, running and looking back, he soon passed out of sight.

When Joseph turned from watching him he

saw Rachel's carriage, now drawn up in front of him; he also saw her stern white face at the carriage window. Then he saw her beckon to him, and with a guilty look he stepped toward the carriage.

Rachel did not speak at first, but her look was more than words. Not until he reached the carriage did she speak, and then she said:

"Get in!"

Without a word, and looking utterly confounded, he opened the door, stepped in, and sat down beside her.

"Drive home!" said Rachel to the driver. And they drove away.

All this Julia saw from her chamber window, and the servants saw it from below.

"Why, that man looked like John!" said Julia to herself. And then she hurried to the *boudoir*. John was not there; nor was Joseph there. She pulled a bell-cord, and when a servant came she asked:

"Where is my husband?"

"He 's gone out, ma'am."

"Where?"

"Do n't know, ma'am; but 't was very queer."

"What was queer?"

"Why his walkin' out so — in his stockin' feet — walkin' on his toes — with his boots in 'is hand."

"What do you mean?"

"That's all ma'am — that's all I seen."

"Do you mean to say that you saw my husband — in his stocking-feet — walking on tip-toe through the house — with his boots in hand?"

"Yes, ma'am."

Julia was stunned.

"You may go," said she; and the servant went away.

"I saw that crazy Pelter across the street, running as if pursued by the seven devils!" reflected Julia. "What was he running for? At the sight of John, no doubt. But why should he run at the sight of John? And who was that white-faced woman sitting in the carriage? And why did John drive away with her? Why did he not speak to me about it? Why did he *steal* away? That looks suspicious!"

Such were Julia's first reflections. Then she sat down to collect her wits and search for some reasonable explanation. In doing this, she searched her place for curiosities, and Mr. Pelter now appeared in her mental panorama.

He seemed singularly associated with all of her perplexities. Was he really crazy? Was not this white-faced woman the one referred to by this strange man in their street encounter? Might not she be the "other wife" of whom he spoke to Thomas? She must have some strong hold on John, to take him from her very arms almost!

Such were Julia's more deliberate reflections; and the more she thought, the more perplexities beset her. At last she started up, with a sudden resolution.

"If John can not explain all this — and to my satisfaction — I will find this Pelter and examine him! But John can and will explain it! He is not a man to prove unfaithful! Yet why did he *steal* away? That is the strangest thing.

She was determined, whatever her suspicions, not to form an adverse judgment before John could have a hearing. With this final resolution, she engaged herself in her affairs.

It was not very far to Joseph's house, and until they reached it neither he nor Rachel spoke. When they were in the house, Rachel turned on Joseph, and with a sneer inquired:

"Can you explain the business of *this* factory?"

Joseph made no reply.

"At last!" said she, "I have caught you, where even your brazen face can not support you in denial!"

"Rachel!" said Joseph, most dejectedly, "give me a little time to collect myself. I have been walking in the mists so long that I can not make things clear, even to myself — much less to you."

"I saw her when she called you to her carriage," answered Rachel; "and after that I followed you. Bear that in mind when you collect yourself, and clear it all!"

Joseph, with a baffled look, went to another room.

"He'll talk no more to me of my suspicious letter, or of Mr. Pelter on his knees!" said Rachel, with a flash of triumph.

CHAPTER VIII.

THE IMP OF DISCORD.

At the usual dinner-hour John came home. Julia met him as she always did, but there was inquiry in her eyes.

"Where are your new clothes?" she asked.

"What?" he answered.

"Why did you not bring home your clothes?"

"What clothes?"

"Why, the ones you wore this morning!"

"These are the ones I wore this morning."

"No, they're not!"

"What's in your head?"

"Well, well; no matter now. Tell me where you went when you left me here."

"Why, I went down town as usual."

"No, no! Not when you *first* went down; but after I had brought you home to lunch!"

"After you had brought me home to lunch!" repeated John, with much astonishment, and looking at his wife.

"Yes. And tell me who that lady was who took you in the carriage with her."

"What sort of quizzing are you at?" asked John; now thinking that his wife was bent on some amusement.

Julia was impatient at what seemed John's attempt to avoid the subject, and she continued, with a serious look: "Come, John! Tell me now. And tell me why you took off your boots and stole away while I was dressing."

"Ha! ha! ha! ho! ho! ho!" laughed John. "Go on! That's good! Took off my boots, and stole away while you were dressing!"

Julia did not join in his amusement, but on the contrary grew more serious; and John soon noticed it.

"Why, Julia, what's the matter with you? You are as incomprehensible as Pelter!"

"Yes; and why was Mr. Pelter here? And what did he run away for?"

John smiled and answered: "Has that crazy fellow been around again? By my faith! Unless you begin to speak more seriously, I shall think that lunacy is infectious, and that Pelter's breath has charged the air. Come, now! be serious, and tell me what you're at!"

"John!" said Julia, now really angry, and flushing as she spoke, "don't treat me in this manner! You know yourself that, to say the least, your actions were very singular; especially your stealing off on tip-toe, and in your stocking-feet, with your boots in hand!"

John could not restrain another laugh at this, and Julia was enraged.

"Why, wife," said John, not knowing what to think, "you speak and look as though you might be in sober earnest!"

"I am in sober earnest, John!" said Julia, almost ready now to cry. "And—I think—you are—*too bad!*"

"Stealing off on tip-toe—and in my stocking-feet!" repeated John, and his laughter threatened to break out again, at the *outre* figure in his mind.

"Why, my dear," said he, "how could I ever do a thing so perfectly ridiculous? And what object could I have in cutting such a figure?"

"Do you deny it?" asked Julia, in great surprise.

"Of course I do! Who told you such a story?"

"Well, I did not see you in *that* condition, but I *did* see you in other situations; and these you cannot deny."

"What other situations?"

"Well, for one, with the woman in the carriage at the door."

"What woman? What carriage?"

"You seem determined to provoke me! You know that I am speaking of the woman who took you off with her!"

"When?"

"To-day!"

"Why, Julia, what 's the matter with you? I have not been off with any woman in a carriage."

"But I saw you!"

"It *is* infectious, I believe!"

"What?"

"Pelter's lunacy."

Julia was furious now, and her eyes snapped fire.

"Perhaps you will deny that you came home with me?"

"When?"

"To-day!"

"How?"

"In the carriage!"

"Of course I *do* deny it, since it 's not the fact."

"And I did not ask you to take me to the theater to-night?"

"I never heard of it before. I shall be very glad to take you there to-night, or any other night when you wish to go."

"What makes you so provoking, John? You do not tell me — seriously, and to my face — that you deny these things?"

"Most certainly I do! Your talk is all as obscure to me as the inscriptions on Egyptian monuments."

"That's all the explanation you intend to give me, is it!"

"It's all I have to give."

"Then you intend to face me down, and openly deny what transpired before my very eyes?"

"There is some mistake! You did not see me, Julia, as you say."

"Enough of this!" said Julia, with a look of dignity. "I find that I have been mistaken in your character."

Then turning on him, with a frown he had never seen before, she added: "Be careful, John, be very careful! I am not a woman to be trifled with, and you will find it so!"

John was so astonished by her tone and anger, that he did not think of stopping her as she now swept proudly from the room.

"Well! upon my word!" he soliloquized, "This has a more serious look than I expected! What curious fancies Julia has! And how they seem to have fixed themselves! They *are* like the phantasies of lunacy! And she clings to them like a madman to his vagaries! No sane mind could ever form an image so superlatively ridiculous as that of my stealing from my house on tiptoe, and in my stocking feet, with my boots in hand! Can it be possible that what I spoke in jest is true, and that this *is* incipient madness? It may result from nervous excitation! but I never dreamed that Julia was so nervous! O, Julia! The apple of my eye! My soul's delight! The object of my constant and increasing love! Can it be possible that some sudden and distressful blight has touched your mind, and that all your sparkling wit has turned to inane phantasies?"

The very thought of such a thing distressed him so acutely that he could think of nothing but some soothing panacea. He resolved to humor, rather than to contradict, her whims, until, from a more thorough observation, he could satisfy himself as to her real condition. With this determination, he went out after her. He found her sitting in another room, with her head bowed on a table, and sobbing convulsively. The sight touched John as no other sight could touch him; and he went up to her, and stooped down and kissed her hair.

"Come, Julia, my darling wife! Do not give way! Look up, and speak to me again! I 'll admit it all! Come now!"

"You admit it, do you?" cried Julia, quickly lifting up her head. "Now explain it to me!"

"First, compose yourself," said John.

Julia rose up in a blaze of jealous passion, and retorted: "You are a sailor, and have often seen the lashes of the wind goad on the swelling waves to fury! Did you ever try to calm them, when they seemed almost to reach the stars, by saying 'compose yourselves'?"

She was wrought up to actual frenzy, and John regarded her with a graver, sadder, and more compassionate expression. He did not know what to say to satisfy and calm her.

"*Did* you, I say," she again broke forth, "ever try to still the waves — or even dream that such a thing was possible—by saying calmly, 'compose yourselves'?"

"No," John answered.

"It would have seemed like folly, would it not?"

"Yes."

"When you can control the coursers of the wind by the bridle of your tongue, then come to me with *such* a tranquilizer as 'compose yourself!' Explanation is what I ask! and that is the *only* thing!"

"When I deny," said John, speaking unconsciously, "she is enraged; when I confess she is absolutely furious! I begin to think that my fears are too well founded, and that she is really going mad!"

"Ha! ha! ha!" laughed Julia in derision. "That's the way you turn it now! Mad! Ha! ha! ha!"

More convinced than ever by her wild, unnatural look and laugh, and unable to control his own emotion, he hurried from the room to conceal his tears.

"He refuses, even yet!" said Julia, now defiant, "and in the very presence of my anguish, to explain himself! Now I believe that he can not explain himself! I will find that Mr. Pelter!"

If Julia had really been demented, she could not have been more entirely possessed by the fancies of her mind than she appeared to be when John next saw her; and John could not have looked more sorrowful and broken had he seen the actual wreck of what was dearer to him than his life. He resolved to consult some eminent authority, and see if something could not be done to restore her faculties.

So the evening and the anxious, sleepless night passed by. On the following morning the situation was unchanged, and John even hastened from the house, so great was his anxiety for a consultation.

Julia was glad to see him go so soon, for she was anxious to commence her search for Mr. Pelter. She ordered the carriage, and at once commenced to dress. When she was ready, the carriage was waiting at the door. She went out, and as she took her seat, said to the coachman:

"Thomas, I must find that queer man Pelter — the man you caught in the barrel-trap. I do n't know who he is, or where he is, and wish you to make some inquiries. If you see him on the street as you drive along, let me know. His name is Pelter."

With this they started off. They did not see Ezekiel on the street, but when they commenced to make their inquiries at different business places, they found that Mr. Pelter was not unknown. Some of the places where they inquired had been deluged with his tracts and charity appeals, and he seemed to have been entirely impartial in his visits to them all; consistency, in this respect, was one of Ezekiel's virtues, and no one could complain of his neglect. Several of those who knew the man did not know his place of residence or where he could be found; but finally, one suggested the Ladies' Missionary Board. With this to guide her in her inquiries, she soon found out where Mr. Pelter lived. She drove to his house, and went herself to ring the bell and make her inquiries.

Mrs. Pelter soon appeared, in answer to the bell, and Julia asked: "Is Mr. Pelter in?"

Here was a woman made of different clay, and formed in a different mould, from that which formed and fashioned those who usually propounded this familiar question, and Mrs. Pelter was really pleased with her appearance; though she wondered all the time what she could want of "Pelter."

"He is out at present," answered Mrs. Pelter.

"I am very sorry," Julia answered. "Can you tell me where I would be most likely to find him?"

"Clinging to some woman's petticoat!" said Mrs. Pelter, spitefully.

Julia smiled. And Mrs. Pelter, seeing it, came as near a smile as she ever did; and, in fact, as near as it was possible to come with such a face as hers.

"What particular petticoat shall I try to find?" asked Julia, with a broader smile.

"Well," said Mrs. Pelter, chuckling at her first conceit, "you'd better go to the brooding-place; you'll probably find them all upon some new egg of mischief."

"Where is that?" inquired Julia, now exceedingly amused.

"At what they call the Ladies' Rooms," said Mrs. Pelter; and she gave the street and number.

Now, for the first time, Julia thought of what John had told her of his visit there, and how she might have saved the trouble of her inquiries if she had thought of it before.

"Is Mr. Pelter wrong in any way up here?" asked Julia, tapping her forehead with her finger.

"What? daft?"

"Yes."

"Why, bless you! No! But I do not wonder that you ask the question; for he is surely a very different man from what he claims to be."

Thanking Mrs. Pelter for her information, and leaving a smile behind to warm the spot where Mrs. Pelter's heart had been, Julia returned to her carriage, and drove away to find the ladies' rooms.

When she reached the "rooms," she sent Thomas in to inquire for Mr. Pelter.

At that very moment the Board was actively engaged in assaults on Julia's character. Ezekiel had just reported to them his observations while with Rachel on the day before. By his spirited remarks he conveyed an impression — unconsciously, perhaps, but he conveyed it — of his unusual dignity and courage on that occasion. He did not even mention — so engaged was he in more important matters — his flying heels in the sight of Joseph Smith.

"Mr. P-e-l-t-e-e-r is inquired for," said a member, returning from the door where Thomas was.

"Who is it?" asked Mr. Pelter.

"He is a coachman — by his dress," the member answered.

Mr. Pelter excused himself, and going to the door, found Thomas there. He stopped in the open door, and did not recognize the coachman.

"Is your name Pelter?" Thomas asked.

"It is," said Mr. Pelter, frowning on this familiarity, and swelling sensibly.

"You look sprucer than you did when we took you from the barrel," continued Thomas, with a merry twinkle in his eye.

"Hush!" said Ezekiel, with his finger up, and then he stepped out and carefully closed the door.

"What is it, my good man?" he now inquired; and, as he spoke, he beamed upon the coachman graciously.

"My mistress wants you."

"Where is she?"

"In her carriage."

"Here?"

"Yes, sir."

Now, it had been the great desire of Ezekiel's secret heart, ever since he saw her first, to make the acquaintance of the "handsome *woo*-man"; and he would in truth much sooner cultivate that blooming garden than the finest moral garden in the world. But these were his secret thoughts, and he was by far too prudent to disclose them to the Board.

"Tell her that I will be out immediately," said he; and he returned.

"Who is it?" asked the members, when he re-appeared.

"The very one we're talking of," said Mr. Pelter.

"Goodness!" exclaimed the members, in surprise. "What does she want?"

"She sent in for me," Ezekiel answered; "she's in her carriage at the door."

Then he added, artfully, — well knowing that he would be urged to go:

"Is it proper?"

"She can't hurt you," said one.

"It is your duty," said a second.

And all, without exception, urged him to go; for they were not disposed, on mere punctilio, to be cheated of a fresh sensation.

"The call of duty," said Ezekiel, bowing to the second member, "always finds its answer here," and he put his hand upon his waistcoat; but really nearer his stomach than his heart — and quite properly. Then he took his broad-brimmed hat and started out.

As he approached the carriage where Julia sat, he lifted off his hat, and let his blandness shine with more than usual splendor.

Julia smiled, and greeted him, and thanked him for his coming.

"Will you get in and ride with me?" said she. "I want to talk with you. I will bring you back again."

Nothing could have been proposed more agreeable to Mr. Pelter, and he showed it in his shining face. With another bow, and without further hesitation, he got in and took a seat beside the handsome "*woo*-man."

"What a world we live in, Mr. Pelter," Julia commenced, as they turned and drove away.

"It is a dying world," said Mr. Pelter, solemnly, and sighing as he spoke.

"What a wicked world it is!" said Julia.

"Oh *what* a wicked world!" responded Mr. Pelter.

"I hope that you did not suffer much from your rough treatment on our grounds on that dark night;" and Julia smiled in spite of all attempts at gravity, as she remembered his appearance then.

"I suffered, madam," replied Ezekiel; "but we were made to suffer."

"How comforting your religion is."

And Julia turned away her head to conceal another smile.

"Oh, it is *such* a comfort! And, madam, I would brave a hundred such dark nights as that to be of service to you."

Here he turned on her his captivating look, and Julia smiled and answered by a word of thanks.

"I want to ask you about that night," continued she. "Tell me why you went there; tell me frankly, Mr. Pelter."

With that fearless look, so natural to him when

he felt secure from danger, he replied: "I went to save you from a godless libertine!"

Julia had not looked, or prepared herself, for such a blast as this, and she was greatly scandalized by a charge so shocking.

"Are you speaking of my husband?" she replied, in a tone of dignified resentment; and in spite of all her own anathemas, her woman's nature would defend the man in whom she trusted once.

"Are you — really — *married* to him?" asked Mr. Pelter, in a tone of great astonishment.

"Do you ask me? Did you not see that we were living there?"

Mr. Pelter saw by her flashing eyes that his awkward feet were treading on torpedoes, and he clumsily attempted to extricate himself.

"Yes," he answered, "I saw that!"

"Then why did you ask me if we were married?"

"Because I did not think that he would dare to go so far."

"Did you think that he would live with me and not be married to me?"

"He might do that!"

"What, then, do you think of me? Am I a wanton? How dare you, sir —"

"Oh no! no! no! I beg ten thousand pardons! I did not think of you! I only thought of him!

Their excited voices reached the coachman's ears, and he turned his head, and saw his mistress glaring on the cowering man. She noticed this, and quickly settled back to her previous position. The coachman, muttering something to himself, turned back to his position.

When Julia spoke again it was almost in a whisper; a nameless and shapeless, but giant and oppressive horror, was coming over her.

"Speak low!" said she, "and tell me what you mean!"

"I mean," said Mr. Pelter, speaking low, "that he has another wife!"

It was a hard and cruel blow, and it fell with crushing weight. Julia sank back, with a smothered moan, and for a moment seemed to be unconscious. Mr. Pelter was alarmed; and he looked with frightened eyes upon the white and deathly face. He was about to have the coachman stop, when Julia, seeing his intention, put her hand upon his arm and shook her head.

Then, by an almost superhuman effort, she threw off the lethargic spell, and leaning over to Ezekiel, whispered:

"Was it the white-faced woman in the carriage, who came for him on yesterday; and who was at the door when I saw you running off?"

"Yes," whispered Mr. Pelter.

"That accounts for her hold on him!" said Julia to herself. Then she continued, speaking to Ezekiel —

"I must see her! Can you arrange it without her knowledge?"

"I think so."

"And can you arrange it so that I can see them both together, think you?"

"Yes; but I must have a little time."

"Will you let me know when it is arranged?"

"Yes."

"Then let me take you back. I must get home! This blow is killing me!"

"Oh, ma'am —" commenced Ezekiel; and then he stopped; for he saw that she did not heed, or even seem to hear him. She aroused herself an instant, and told the coachman to take Mr. Pelter back, and then drive home. After this, she sank back again, and closed her eyes, and did not move or speak until the carriage stopped for Mr. Pelter to get out.

Then she sat up, and with her hand on Mr. Pelter's arm, and her face near his, she said impressively: "Remember! you must let me know!"

"I will," said Mr. Pelter.

Standing by the curb-stone, he watched the carriage as it drove away, and the image of that white, distressful face, was fixed upon his mind forever.

"Another heart is broken by that wicked man!" said he; not dreaming that he himself had caused all the mischief.

When Julia reached her home she found her husband there, and a stranger whom she had never seen before.

John was so shocked by her appearance when she entered that he could not control his mastering emotions; and he broke down with sobs, and hurried to a private room to regain composure.

The stranger, with a look of tenderness and pity, stepped up to Julia, and said to her, "Let me assist you to your room."

She could not refuse his proffered help, for she was too weak to reach her room unaided. Hanging on the stranger's arm, and looking in his kind and sympathizing face, she asked:

"Are you John's friend?"

"Yes, and yours," he answered.

"I am glad of that," said she; "for it seems a very heavy blow to him."

"It is, indeed," the stranger answered.

"His sobs," said Julia, "fell like heavy hammers on my heart. I thought that I should hate him — but — I can't — I can't!"

By this time they had reached her room, and

" Are you John's friend ? "

as soon as her wrappings were removed the stranger helped her to a sofa, where she reclined.

John appeared directly after. He took a chair and drew it up to Julia's side, and reached out to take her hand.

She drew her hand away. "Which one was first?" she asked in a languid tone.

A sharp, quick glance was instantly exchanged between the husband and the stranger, as they heard the question.

"Which one was *first* I ask?" repeated Julia. "Don't you understand me?"

"No," said John. "What do you mean?"

"Which one did you marry first?"

Another look was here exchanged between the husband and the stranger.

"Was *she* the first?" persisted Julia.

"Yes, yes," said John, not knowing what to say.

"It is better so than the other way," continued Julia.

"How?" asked John.

"Why, I would rather be the one who holds your heart — and I believe I do — even if our marriage was unlawful, than to be the deserted wife!"

A moment's silence intervened, and then she spoke again:

"But, John, it was a very wicked thing to

do! I think—I know indeed—that you did not dream that it would cost your Julia's life; but —it will!"

Another painful silence passed, and she again continued:

"I can never show my face again! It is such a shame! It will be very hard for me to give you up: but I must do it. You belong to her!"

Here the stranger interrupted, saying, "You will feel better for a little rest. I am a physician; let me give you something. When you have had a little sleep we can talk of all these things."

"It is a healer of the soul *I* need," responded Julia. "This physical machinery is of very little value to me now; and I do not care how soon the wheels run down—and—stop!"

While she was speaking, the doctor took some medicine from a little pocket-case, and as soon as she had finished he offered it to her.

"Take it!" said he; "you will feel better for it."

"To please you I will take it, for you are kind; but for myself, I do not care."

She took the medicine. The effect was very soon apparent. Her breathing was more natural and her system generally more relaxed. Soon her eyes grew dull and heavy; and then they closed; and then her soft, low breath gave notice of her slumber.

The stranger was an eminent physician, and one who gave particular attention to treatments of the "mind diseased." John had been with him since he first found him in the morning. He repeated to the doctor his strange interview with Julia.

"That fancy of my walking in my stocking-feet, and stealing from her, seems to trouble her the most of anything," said John. "But yet she is just as earnest and as positive in the declaration that I went home to lunch with her, and was carried off from there by some white-faced woman."

"Is there not some foundation for these fancies?" asked the doctor.

"Not the least!" said John, most positively. "So far was she from taking me to lunch as this; I did not even see her during the entire day! And I certainly did not go off with any woman — white-faced or black, or of any other color. As to my walking on my toes in my stocking-feet, and stealing from the house in such a way, it is too ridiculous to be reconciled with sanity."

"Well, I will go with you, and see her," said the doctor.

"What do you think from what I've said to you?" asked John, with manifest anxiety.

"You may be right," the doctor answered. "I am inclined to think you are. But do not be cast down; it may be — and, indeed, is likely to be — merely a temporary aberration, resulting from some physical disorder, which may very soon be regulated.

So they started for the house. When they reached the house, Julia was away. The servants did not know where she had gone, and they sat down to wait for her return. When she did return, they did not see her until she entered.

As soon as Julia was asleep, the doctor suggested that they retire to another room, and ascertain, if possible, where she had been, and how employed while she was out. "It may lead us," the doctor said, "to something more determinate."

They retired to another room, and John stepped out and sent for Thomas, who very soon appeared.

"This gentleman," said John to him, "will state some questions to you; I wish you to answer them carefully and frankly."

Thomas bowed and gave his attention to the doctor.

"Where have you been this morning, and how has your mistress been engaged?" the doctor asked.

"We have been hunting for a queer old chap by the name of Pelter," Thomas answered, "and when we found him she had a talk with him."

"What did they talk about?"

"I did not hear; but once or twice my mistress was very much excited; and she seemed, somehow, broke down when Pelter left us. Then I drove home."

"Is that all?"

"That's all, sir."

"You may go," said John, and Thomas at once retired.

"Who is this Pelter? Do you know him?" asked the doctor, turning to John.

"Well," said John, "*he* is a crazy fellow, or a very foolish one; and I did not think to state before that he seems to be, somehow, mixed up in the confusion of her mind. She asked me why he ran away when the woman took me off."

Here John told all he knew of Mr. Pelter, and closed by saying: "He seems to be so fixed in her curious fancies, that it is not strange, perhaps, that she should try to find him. In a sound and healthy state of mind, she could have no earthly object in seeing him."

"You see," remarked the doctor, "by what she said just now, that she has other fancies than those you stated; and that the one now prominent with her is that you have another wife, whom you have deserted."

"Yes," said John, "and that was one of Pelter's crazy notions."

"Then," said the doctor, "he may have conveyed that impression to your wife. Here is a starting point, at all events."

"Yes, and a stopping point!" said John, speaking with excitement. "If I find him hanging around my house again I will order his arrest!"

"I am not satisfied upon the question of your wife's condition," said the doctor, "and must talk with her. We can do no more at present. She will sleep for several hours, perhaps, and when she wakens she may be more clear, or — she may not."

"What do you mean when you say that she may not?"

"Well, it is possible that this excitement and anxiety may terminate in some serious affection of the brain, of which her present state is the inception; if so, it is quite likely that all these fancies are really the images produced by physical disease, as I said before, and that they will vanish, and be remembered only as a dream — and a shadowy one at that — when she recovers. Now I must go. You can send for me when her sleep is over." With this, the doctor went away, and left the frightened and bewildered John with the specters of his fears.

Julia's sleep was not so long or so profound as the doctor thought it would be; and when John returned to her, he found her restless and turning on her couch, and muttering incoherent words. The fever had begun, and her heated blood was swelling all her veins by its rapid and unnatural flow. Her face and hands were hot and dry; and when she started from her sleep, and John offered her some water, she clutched the glass with trembling fingers and drained it eagerly. Then she settled back, with a long-drawn breath, and fixed her eyes on John. But he could see that her look was vacant; and when he spoke to her, and she commenced to speak again, he saw that her mind was wandering.

The doctor had scarcely reached his office when he was called, and hurried back again.

"This is what I said might happen," said he to John, after seeing Julia.

"But is there danger?" inquired John, in a frightened tone.

"No immediate danger," replied the doctor, "and perhaps no real danger; for she will have every care. In all such cases, there is much in proper care. In her intervals of consciousness — if she has them, and probably she will not — try to tranquilize her mind, and never try to settle vexing questions. Nature is the great physician now, and much depends on constant watchfulness and careful nursing."

The doctor then wrote out prescriptions, and gave all necessary orders, and went away again. John nerved himself for the coming fight with death.

CHAPTER IX.

MR. PELTER AS A STAR.

AFFAIRS at Joseph's house were in a sad condition. Confidence was entirely destroyed between himself and Rachel. Each felt guilty of a guiltless indiscretion; and each felt properly indignant that the indiscretion was so magnified. Neither could charge the other without receiving a counter-charge, and each believed the other to be more guilty than a knowledge of the actual facts would justify.

Joseph tried to introduce the subject and come to mutual explanations; but Rachel would not be satisfied with this, and required from him, first, the confession of a crime which existed only in her jealous fancy.

"You do not exercise that charity which, as a Christian woman, you should exercise," said Joseph.

"Nor do you practice those Christian virtues which you should practice!" retorted Rachel.

"Your religion, then, is not a help in time of need," continued Joseph.

"It is too much like yours!" again retorted Rachel,—"confined to preaching more than practice."

Thus, their anger stripped the masks from off their faces, and left no common ground to stand upon. Sullenly, angrily, and defiantly, they took their separate courses.

Joseph, after this, was much absent from his home. Rachel, believing that she knew *where* he was, was more and more possessed by jealousy and hate.

"If I can catch them in a public place, I'll expose them to the world," said she.

Joseph's evenings now were nearly always spent away from home, and he established new associations, to fill his leisure hours. This unfortunate estrangement drove Rachel more and more to the "Ladies' Rooms." The Board received her as a victim; and they never tired of increasing her uneasiness by artful innuendoes.

Mr. Pelter was constantly upon the watch to hit upon some time and place when he would be certain of finding Joseph and his wife together, that he might communicate the fact to Julia; but the unfortunate estrangement defeated all his plans.

Affairs remained in this condition until Julia had passed the crisis of her malady, and had convalesced, and finally recovered. The attack had been as severe and dangerous, as it was sudden and unexpected. For many hours, at its turning-point, she was shadowed by the hovering wings of death. But she rallied—feebly first, and then with greater strength—until, with conscious smiles, she chased the shadows from the room.

John, worn by watching and anxiety, was the object of her first wondering gaze. Her low voice struck him like an electric shock, as she inquired, "How is this?"

"O! my DARLING!" was all that he could say; and he bowed his head upon the bed, while great sobs choked him. She put her wasted hand upon his head, and by that simple touch filled him with her tenderness.

"Have I been so ill?" she asked.

Now John looked up, and a great beatitude was shining through his tears.

"Why, John, you look worn out!" said she. "Have I been here long?"

"Oh! so long! An eternity! if duration can be counted by our throbs of anguish."

"How you love me, John." And here she took his hand and smiled.

"I never knew how much till now!"

"I am trying to remember; it is like a hideous nightmare; I can't make it out."

"Don't try to make it out!" cried John, with eagerness.

"I must try, John. My mind will work in spite of me; and it is better to settle its perplexities than to leave it in a muddle. Some well-intentioned people have strange notions as to the proper treatment of a curious mind. In mistaken kindness, they refuse to answer questions, and drive it back upon itself, to fret and worry, until, in new perplexities, it finds itself distracted. Do n't treat me this way. Has my brain been touched? Have I been wandering?"

"Yes," said John, converted to her notion of a proper treatment.

"That explains it then!" said she, with a sigh of visible relief. "I have had some curious fancies, John. I saw that crazy Pelter; and I saw a white-faced woman take you off from me. Even now these forms are so distinct as to seem realities. They *are* fancies, are they not? I did not really see them, did I? And yet I could almost swear to their existence!"

"They are all delusions!" answered John. "Depend upon it! I am not deceiving you!" Nor did he think he was.

"Well then," said Julia, "let us banish them!" With this, she marshaled all her fancies in a ghostly line, then linked them to what she now believed to be the image of the white-faced woman, and drove them from her brain. With this came rest. With rest came strength. With strength came thankfulness and joy. Sunshine filled the house again; and Julia's songs and laughter startled all the specters from their crannies.

John was determined to protect his wife against a recurrence of distressful scenes. He gave to Thomas most particular and positive instructions. "If," said he, "that fellow Pelter comes about the house again, you must arrest him, and hand him over to the authorities. I will bear you out in it, and will appear and make the proper charges. Julia's life is too precious to me to be again endangered."

"He shall not escape if I catch him here again," said Thomas.

Rachel was urged, from time to time, by the Ladies' Board, to commence proceedings against her husband, by a criminal complaint; but she could not be induced to go so far as that. She was always on the watch to secure proofs of Joseph's guilt; but she could not lend herself to a prosecution, which would, she thought, result in his imprisonment for a term of years.

Mr. Pelter, after being baffled for a score of times in his efforts to determine when he would be certain of finding Joseph at home with Rachel, at last resolved upon a more direct attempt. When he next met Rachel at the "rooms," he asked: "When *is* your husband home?"

"Usually at dinner," answered Rachel. "All other times are most uncertain now."

When he heard this answer, he accused himself of great stupidity for not thinking of that himself. He knew that the windows of the dining-room opened toward the street, and near enough to enable a passer-by — especially if sitting in a carriage — to see distinctly objects in the room. He could not hit upon a better plan than was at once suggested.

"We can catch them at the dinner-table!" he reflected, "and without the danger of discovery, by simply driving past. But he can 't be there *every* day to dinner; for some days he must be with the other *woo*-man!"

"He is not there *every* day to dinner, is he?" he continued, speaking audibly.

"No; he is often absent," Rachel answered.

"She 'll know," reflected Mr. Pelter, "when he is absent, for he 'll be with her!"

Some little time had passed since Julia called on him, and he was impatient to see and talk with her again. He had no knowledge of her sickness, or of the sad effects of his previous disclosures; and before he had settled on his present plan for finding Joseph and his wife together, she was well again. A few days after he had settled on this plan, he set out for Julia's house, to advise her of it.

He was dressed with unusual care, and was determined on making a most favorable impression. When he was near the house he stooped to dust his feet, and his shining face was reflected in his polished boots. He concluded not to ring the bell, for he might thus attract attention and curiosity, and he walked past the house, with his eyes upon the windows. He hoped to see Julia there, but did not, and so he turned and walked back again. Back and forth he walked again, and then again, looking at the windows, until the servants noticed him.

Julia was not at home, and the servants, thinking that such conduct had a suspicious look, hurried to the stable, and reported to the coachman. They described the man, and Thomas in an instant, thought of the "crazy Pelter," and of John's instructions with regard to him.

"Let me see," said he, and he stooped and craned his neck, and carefully looked out from the stable door — his body not exposed. The girls, on tip-toe, looked above his head, ready, at an instant's warning, to dodge out of sight.

Mr. Pelter, in his repeated walks, not seeing Julia, resorted to another means of attracting her attention. He took out his large and spotless handkerchief, and put it to his nose, and then with all his might blew such a blast as nearly shook the windows in their frames.

" He blew such a blast as nearly shook the windows in their frames."

"G-r-a-c-i-o-u-s! what a nose!" the girls exclaimed, and then they tittered. Here Mr. Pelter came in sight, walking majestically and looking at the windows.

"That's him! that's him!" the girls cried out, and then retreated from the door.

"Yes," said Thomas, also dodging back, "that's the fellow — sure!"

"Who?" asked the girls, excited.

"Why, the thief we caught here — in the barrel," answered Thomas, chuckling, as he noticed their look of fear.

"Mercy!" cried the girls, in real alarm, "he's taking observations for another visit! Probably he knows that mistress is away, and thinks you gone as well."

"For all his dress, he has a villain's look!" said one.

"Yes," the other said, "and a savage villain's look." And their imaginations made him quite a furious monster, when, in fact, he would have run in terror from either one of them.

"Stand back! stand back!" said Thomas, "I must manage to get him in here somehow."

"In here! To cut our throats? Wait, Tom! Wait! Let us get out!" exclaimed the girls; and then they ran until they reached the house, and shut and locked the door.

Thomas now walked out, as though unconscious

of Mr. Pelter's presence. By this time Ezekiel had made his usual turn, and walked back again. Thomas was near the fence when he came back. Mr. Pelter saw him, and, in his loftiest and most patronizing tone, he said:

"Ah! how *are* you?"

"How are *you?*" Thomas answered.

"Thanks to a gracious Providence, I am well — very well," said Mr. Pelter.

"Will you walk in and see the grounds?" asked Thomas, pleasantly; for he feared that Mr. Pelter might escape if he tried to catch him on the street.

"Ahem!" said Mr. Pelter, pleased with the suggestion, and thinking that he would be certain now of Julia's notice. "Thank you, I will step in a moment."

Thomas held the gate for him, and he stepped in and began to admire a bed of flowers near.

"Do you ever think, my man," said he, with unction, "of the Giver of these bright flowers?"

"They was n't give to us; my mistress bought 'em at the green-house."

Ezekiel groaned.

"Come and see the stable," continued Thomas.

"Here! read this!" said Mr. Pelter, holding out what he had just taken from his pocket.

"What's that?" asked Thomas, looking at it.

Ezekiel put his finger on the head-lines of his

favorite tract, and read out the words, in his lofty and impressive tone:

"Beware of the Wrath to Come."

"All right," said Thomas, and he again invited Mr. Pelter to the stable.

"If I could only call you to the manger!" Ezekiel fervently exclaimed.

"They 're all out of date!" said Thomas, "We feed from racks and boxes now! Come! I 'll show you."

"Too true! Too true!" said Ezekiel solemnly.

"What 's too true?"

"That the manger is all out of date! O! what a world!"

"As crazy as a loon!" said Thomas to himself.

By this time they had reached the stable, and Thomas stood aside for Ezekiel to enter. As soon as Thomas entered, he looked about and found a stout but slender piece of rope; then approaching Mr. Pelter from behind, he caught his arms and drew them back, and in a twinkle tied them.

"Now," said he, "I 've got you!"

Mr. Pelter was so overcome by fear, at first, that he was speechless; and Thomas, taking advantage of his condition, quickly placed him in position and strapped his legs, and then his body to a post.

"You must excuse me," said the coachman, while at work, "and call out if I draw too hard. I would not tie you, but I must fix you sure, so I can leave you while I get ready to take you off."

Mr. Pelter thought of abduction, torture, assassination, and a hundred other frightful things; for Joseph's threats to Mrs. Pelter were running in his mind.

Trembling from head to foot, and stammering in his speech, he asked:

"Wh — wh — where?"

"To the police station," Thomas answered.

Ezekiel's courage mounted now, and he no longer trembled, for the thought of danger to his person was removed. The idea of a brief confinement for the sake of righteousness was rather pleasing than *dis*pleasing to his mind. He had twanged so long upon a single string, that the familiar sound was irksome even to himself. This arrest, if properly manipulated, would furnish him another string, and he would strike such wailing sounds from it as to reach hearts insensible to his usual appeals.

In imagination, he could already see the indignant members of the Board hurling thunderbolts against his prison-walls; and even Mrs. Pelter must be touched to some compassion by his distress. Rachel, and "My-*rindy*," and the "handsome *woo*-man," would all regard him with a higher veneration than before, when they saw him suffering in their cause. And what an endless theme for tracts! He would write, and throw them from between his prison bars, as thick and fast as snowflakes come in a winter storm! He luxuriated in these thoughts; and now he only feared that he might be discharged, and not confined at all.

Thomas, when he had "fixed him sure," went in to notify the servants in the house, and offer them a chance to look upon his prisoner.

"Are you sure," they asked, "that you have him safe?"

"As safe as a thief in stocks!" said he.

With this assurance, they ventured to the stable, following in the coachman's wake. With hesitating steps, when they reached the door, they entered.

Mr. Pelter's clothing was disarranged somewhat, by the trussing Thomas gave him. His breeches-legs were drawn up above his boot-tops, and his hat, by contact with the post, was knocked upon one side. This gave him a rakish look, which detracted much from the impressiveness of what he very gravely uttered. He looked, in truth, more like a drunken man, attempting to convince you of his sobriety, than like himself, the peerless Mr. Pelter. His appearance, instead of appealing to the compassion of the servants, amused them greatly, and they nudged each other and tittered, and then laughed outright, Thomas joining them.

"Did your master order this assault upon my liberties?" inquired Mr. Pelter, in a crushing tone.

"It 's strictly 'cordin' to instructions," answered Thomas, with a smile.

"You're a child of sin!" said Mr. Pelter, as he noticed Thomas' smile, "with no bowels of compassion!"

In his earnestness he threw back his head, and hit his hat again against the post, knocking it to a new position, more rakish than before. At this the servants laughed again, and Thomas joined them. One eye now was nearly covered by his hat, and with that half open, and the other fairly blazing with his indignation, he gave them such a look as he thought would crush them, but it only served to increase their irreverent merriment.

Thomas now retired to make some changes in his dress, and the servants scampered to the house again.

"Now, old chap," said Thomas, on his return, "if you'll be quiet, and not try to get away, I 'll take all your fastenings off."

"I will go with you," the good man answered, and this was all that he would say.

On this parole Thomas untied him from the post and freed his hands.

"Come on!" said Thomas, and they started off. Ezekiel was silent, but there was a dignified serenity upon his face. When they reached the station-house Thomas gave him up to the authorities.

"What is the complaint?" asked the officer.

"General cussedness!" Thomas anwered.

"But why did you arrest him?"

"Actin' under orders."

"Whose orders?"

"My master's; I will go and bring him."

Without waiting for another word, Thomas went out to report to John.

"What is the name of the man who ordered your arrest?" asked the officer of Mr. Pelter.

"Joseph Smith," replied Ezekiel, and the name of Joseph Smith was duly written in the records.

"What is your name?"

With a pardonable degree of pride, and some pomposity, Ezekiel replied: "Pelter, sir—Ezekiel Pelter—of the Missionary Board!"

His name was also written in the records; and Ezekiel was astonished to observe that neither his name nor that of the Missionary Board, seemed to make the least impression on the officer.

Taking down a bunch of keys hanging near his desk, the officer rose, and said to Mr. Pelter: "Come this way."

Mr. Pelter followed him, and was transferred to less cheerful quarters, where, for the present, he was left without confinement in a cell. The officer retired, and locked the door behind him.

"Hold there!" cried Mr. Pelter, from a grated opening in the door.

The officer stopped and turned around, and Mr. Pelter said:

"I must advise my friends of my situation. Will you give me pen, and ink, and paper?"

The officer nodded and walked on. He soon returned with pen, and ink, and paper, and handed them to Mr. Pelter through the grated opening in the door. Until now Ezekiel had not looked about him. There were other prisoners in the open room or hall-way where he was left; and in nearly all of the diamond openings in the doors of cells around he saw curious and sometimes vicious faces. Those in the hall-way with him soon came up and questioned him, with jeers, and grimaces, and boisterous laughter. Their faces and their language were so repulsive and terribly profane, and Ezekiel was so shocked by the association, that he drew away and sat down by a small rough table, and commenced his letters to his friends. The others left him for a time, and only among themselves made comments on his looks.

One letter was to the ladies of the Board, and another to Mrs. Pelter.

The one to the ladies of the Board is yet preserved, and curious readers are referred to it as a matchless specimen of Mr. Pelter's masterly descriptions. It was read by the Austere Member; and the awful stillness of the room was only broken by the moans of Miranda Trap and the sobs of the other members. Ezekiel was compared to the Apostle Paul in *his* imprisonment; and the comparison was most decidedly in favor of the Christian soldier of the Board. It is undoubtedly the fact that in luxuriant imagery and sublime self-centering the apostle was eclipsed.

Mrs. Pelter read her letter with far different feelings.

"It serves him right," said she; "though I must try and get him out. Perhaps this will teach him to let other people regulate their own affairs!"

In due time Thomas returned, accompanied by John.

"Is this Mr. Smith?" inquired the officer.

"It is," John answered.

"What is the charge against this man Pelter?"

"I hardly know what the technical offense would be, but I will state the facts."

John then proceeded to relate how Mr. Pelter had been caught in his grounds at night, prying about the house; and how, as Thomas had informed him, he was taking other observations when arrested.

"The fellow is a thief, no doubt," the officer remarked.

"He has a very pious way of talking," interrupted Thomas.

"Oh, that's a favorite dodge with some," replied the officer, with a knowing smile. "The devil's 'livery of heaven' is among his favorite costumes; he dresses preachers in it sometimes."

"When will it be necessary for me to come and testify?" inquired John.

"Well," said the officer, "he will first receive a preliminary examination before a justice; then he will be bound over for his trial. Your man, here, knows all the facts, and for the purpose of the examination his testimony will be sufficient. We will not really need you until the trial in the higher court; of that we will send you notice. Let your man be here to-morrow, and testify at the examination."

With these instructions John and Thomas went away.

Then the officer took down his bunch of keys, and went in to Mr. Pelter.

"Here, my man," said he, with his hand on Ezekiel's shoulder, "you belong in separate quarters."

Saying this, he took Ezekiel to an empty cell, and opened it, and shut Ezekiel in. The dark and unclean place did not correspond at all with Mr. Pelter's previous notions; and the idea of a confinement here was much less attractive than before.

The Board made inquiries, and ascertained that he would be examined on the following morning. They resolved to support him by their presence and encouragement. They were present at the opening of the court on the following day, but the place was not attractive, and they were shocked to see their respected member in the crowded dock, surrounded by the moral offal of the city.

When Mr. Pelter saw them, his heavy heart plucked courage from their presence, and he looked upon the court with much complacency, from a moral pinnacle.

His wife was much more practical than the members of the Board, in what she did. As soon as she was notified of his confinement, she went for legal counsel. She was advised, among other things, that her husband could be released on bail, even if he should be held for trial. She took this information to Ezekiel at the station-house, and sent the lawyer to consult with him. So, when the case was called, he had counsel for his defense.

But the story of the coachman was so simple and direct, and so free from ambiguity and contradiction, that the court could not do otherwise than hold Ezekiel for trial. He was so held, and his bail was fixed at a reasonable amount. He was now transferred from the station-house to the city prison.

The story of the coachman, when he gave his testimony as to Mr. Pelter's conduct when he was trapped on that unlucky night, was so entirely different from the impression made by Mr. Pelter in *his* account of it, that the members of the Board were unanimous in the opinion that the prosecution was supported by false testimony; and this increased their indignation.

"Joseph Smith," said they, "is trying to destroy the character of Mr. Pelter, and fix a crime upon him, that he may be secure from Mr. Pelter's charges!"

This was a sufficient motive, in the opinion of the Board, to induce the guilty man to resort to perjury in the present case; and they now urged Rachel more strongly than before to take some active measures in opposition to her husband.

"Next he will commence upon yourself!" said they, "and try to hide *your* knowledge behind prison walls."

"If he should ever even think of such a thing," said Rachel, in a burst of passion, "I will prosecute to the bitter end! But he dare not think of such a thing. I intend to speak to him of Mr. Pelter's matter, for I will not have him prosecute that man for acting in my service!"

This resolution was applauded with enthusiasm, and Rachel was so aroused that she determined to go in person to the city prison, and assure the persecuted man of her active sympathy, and her intentions as to his release. The Austere Member volunteered to go with her.

As Mr. Pelter was being conducted from the court-room, he saw his wife. In a quiet and unostentatious way, she approached him, and, with other words of comfort, said that she would take immediate measures to secure bail, and that his confinement would be brief. This, coming as it did from one so energetic as his wife, was all that Mr. Pelter needed to assure content. Now he was himself again — dignified and bland. To have seen him walking with the sheriff to the city prison, a stranger would have thought that the officer had been guilty of some grave offense, and that Mr. Pelter was trying to console him by some hopeful prospect.

When they reached the prison, Mr. Pelter masked his look of satisfaction behind an outward show of great solemnity. He was a martyr now, and his look and words must support the character.

His present quarters, in comparison with his previous ones, seemed almost cheerful; and he looked around — in spite of his solemnity — with a glance of satisfaction.

"Where are your chains?" he asked, with the tone and look of that provincial favorite in tragedy before referred to.

"Chains!" replied the sheriff, in surprise.

"Bring them on!" continued Mr. Pelter, loftily, "and I will show you how a Christian bears his persecutions."

Believing that his confinement would be brief, he wished to make the most of it; and if he could really wear the clanking chains, his imprisonment would prove a mine of wealth to him, since his quick imagination could then invest the situation with tragic horrors impossible to invent if he was treated kindly.

"Chains are only used on desperate criminals," the sheriff answered. And the answer only served to stimulate Ezekiel's desire to wear them. To be treated as a desperate criminal would be to glorify his martyrdom.

"My enemies will not be satisfied if my limbs

are free! Put on the chains!" insisted Mr. Pelter.

"It would be contrary to our regulations," the sheriff still protested.

"Will you bring them to me and let me see them?" asked Ezekiel.

"Well, it is a curious and unusual request," the sheriff answered, "but I will let you see them if you wish."

Leaving Mr. Pelter in the corridor, and smiling at the odd request, the sheriff went out and soon returned with the clanking chains.

"There they are," said the sheriff, dropping them on the solid floor of stone, "and it is a style of jewelry not usually admired."

The clanking sound struck Mr. Pelter's ears like music, and made him more than ever anxious to have on the chains. What an object for compassion he would be! Here they were interrupted by a call, and the sheriff hurried out to answer it. For the remainder of the day he was so engaged that the thought of Mr. Pelter and his chains did not occur to him.

As soon as the sheriff had retired, Mr. Pelter lifted up the chains and examined them. One of them was the arms, and connected two broad iron bands, fitted for the wrists. These, when properly secured, were firmly riveted. The other one connected broader and heavier bands, formed to clasp the ankles. These also, when properly secured, were firmly riveted. After he had examined them, he tried them on. To secure them, he sacrificed his spotless handkerchief; he tore it into strips, and passing these through the rivet-holes, he contrived to tie them with his fingers and his teeth, so as to hold the bands in place. Then he walked along the corridor and dragged the heavy chain upon the sounding floor until the other prisoners, confined in cells, looked out and watched him with amazement as he passed their doors.

Then he practiced for awhile, in impressive attitudes, and would hold his chained hands up before imaginary witnesses. But at length he tired of this, and untied the bands and released himself. He then began an examination of his prison.

The corridor in which the sheriff left him extended along the side, and was lighted by two large windows, beneath one of which was a narrow table and a single chair. The windows were made secure by means of heavy iron bars, placed at short distances from each other, and firmly bedded in the solid masonry of the heavy prison walls. Opening on the corridor was a row of cells, and he now, for the first time, noticed that most of them were occupied. The walls, and floor, and cells were all of heavy stone, and the doors were iron-studded, and hung on massive iron hinges, and secured by iron bolts. From little diamond openings in the doors of cells, prisoners looked out curiously, wondering who this strange man was. He did not speak to them, but, shrouded in solemnity, and looking on the floor, he walked back and forth.

At last he sat down by the narrow table, and began to arrange his thoughts for projected tracts and pamphlets. In such employments the day passed by. When it was nearly night the jailer entered and informed the distinguished prisoner that some ladies wished to see him.

"Who are they?" he asked.

The jailer handed him their cards.

"Rachel! and a member of the Board!" he exclaimed, with some excitement. "Can I see them here!"

"Oh, yes," the jailer answered.

"Give me a little time to compose myself."

"How long?"

"Ten minutes."

"All right." And with this reply the jailer went to notify the visitors.

The chains were more than ever tempting now, and Mr. Pelter, without reflecting that he would be practicing a deception, commenced to put them on.

"This will touch their hearts!" said he, as he tied the strings.

Then he sat down again, with one elbow on the table and the other hand upon his knee; the chain extending from the upright wrist to the hand upon the table. By the time he had arranged all this, and reclined his head upon his upright hand, the jailer entered, escorting Rachel and the Austere Member of the Board.

The jailer was as much surprised as the ladies were, to see Ezekiel in chains; and his puzzled look was almost comical. As soon as Mr. Pelter saw them, he rose, and, by an artful movement, caused the chains to rattle. Then he slowly stepped toward the visitors, and the heavy clank! clank! clank! upon the sounding floor caused them to stop and gaze in speechless wonder on the spectacle. The jailer, no less stupefied than they, wondered how and why the prisoner had secured and donned these grim and heavy trappings.

Mr. Pelter was in secret ecstacies, as he beheld the profound effect of his manœuvre; but he was careful that his face should not disclose his feelings.

Rachel felt she had brought him to this distressful plight, and her self-reproaches and accusings were unsparing. With tears and protestations she assured Ezekiel that she would not rest until she had effected his release. The Austere Member was too indignant for any such

Mr. Pelter as a star.

expression. In her righteous anger, she threatened to bring down the wrath of God and man upon the heads of those who were guilty of the outrage.

"*He* suffered," said Ezekiel, with a look of noble resignation, which called forth a burst of admiration from the visitors: "and," continued he, "He forgave His enemies." Now he raised one hand — with a clanking of the chain — and his blandness played like celestial light around.

"In charity and kindness speak for me," he again continued; "but only so; for — I forgive — them — all!"

Here was an exaltation in the moral heights never reached by Ezekiel before; and the member stood in silent awe before him.

"Leave me now," said he, in a tone of tender sadness. "Leave me to my meditations."

"Bless you, sir!" said Rachel, with emotion.

"O! Mr. P-e-l-t-e-e-r!" sobbed the Austere Member.

Incapable of further speech, they sadly turned away, and left him to his meditations. And as they went, the clank! clank! clank! of the heavy chain upon the sounding floor followed after them, until the iron-studded door had shut them from the prison walls.

With their exit from the stage, the actor's part was done.

He had just untied the iron bands, and released himself, when the jailer reappeared.

"What is all this nonsense?" the jailer asked.

"Do you call it nonsense?" Mr. Pelter answered, with pretended indignation.

"Shut up! you sanctimonious humbug! Don't try to come it over me! How did you get those things?"—pointing to the chains upon the floor.

"The sheriff brought them in."

"What! For you to strut and work on people's feelin's with?"

"No; for me to look at."

"I have more than half a mind to put them on in earnest, and *then* see how you'll enjoy it."

"Oh no! Don't do that!"

"You're a cunning scamp! But I'll put a stop to this high-tragedy!"

With this, he took up the chains, and said to Mr. Pelter, "Come this way! It's time to lock you up." Saying this, he took him to a cell and locked him in.

Thus the act abruptly closed; with the Star behind the drop.

At a later hour, the laughing stars of heaven peeped forth from behind *their* curtain, and through the window and the diamond opening in the door of Ezekiel's cell, winked their shining eyes at him, as though they had enjoyed the scene. Ezekiel was content.

CHAPTER X.

THE WHITE-FACED WOMAN IN THE TOILS.

JOHN said nothing to his wife of Ezekiel's arrest, for he feared that any mention of the man might raise the ghosts so hard to lay.

She was now entirely restored, and John was more than ever anxious to contribute to her pleasure, and fill their evening hours with agreeable amusements.

When the curtain dropped on Mr. Pelter's play in the city prison, hundreds were making ready for the rising curtain at a favorite theater, which promised on that night unusual attractions. John and Julia were among the number so making ready.

Rachel and the Austere Member were preparing for another act in the tragi-comedy wherein *they* were acting. They resolved to see and talk with Joseph as to Mr. Pelter's persecution and, if possible, to make him join them in active efforts for Ezekiel's release. To make sure of finding him as soon as possible, they went to his usual business places, but it was so late that they did not find him. It was quite late when they made their final inquiry, and they were tired. So they found a place where they could rest and refresh themselves.

After they had rested and refreshed themselves, and when they were about to start for home, they were astonished to discover how late it was.

"I declare! it's nearly eight o'clock!" said the Austere Member.

"So late!" said Rachel; then we can do nothing more to-night.

"No," said the member; and they started off to find a conveyance home. They took a stage. As they passed the theater where the unusual attraction was announced, Rachel caught the member's arm, and in a quick, excited voice, cried out:

"Look!"

"Where?" asked the member.

But Rachel did not hear, for she had already pulled the strap, and was getting out. The member followed her. Rachel caught her arm, and hurried with her to the pavement; she did not stop until she had reached the side of the entrance to the theater. They were none too soon.

John and Julia almost touched their garments

as they passed them. Julia was radiant to-night, and while they were in Rachel's sight, she gave John a coquettish tap with her flashing fan, and such a smile as made Rachel writhe in jealous tortures. The throng soon closed around John and Julia, and they disappeared within.

"I saw them getting from a carriage before I left the stage!" said Rachel, almost breathless with excitement.

"Going to a theater!" exclaimed the member, in a tone of pious horror.

"Yes, and with his mistress!" Rachel answered, with a hiss of rage.

"Is she the one—the one he lives with?" asked the member quickly.

"Yes," said Rachel, starting forward. "Now come with me! I must go in! We cannot wait here! I must see them when they come out! I'll expose them *here!* in this public place!"

The member was most willing to avail herself of this excuse to visit the forbidden precincts of a theater, and they went in together.

The member's eyes began to wander in delight around the house; and she could not but think how much more attractive every thing appeared than in the gloomy places of rectangular enjoyment to which she was accustomed.

Is it any wonder that pleasure finds more votaries than the chilling pageantries of woe? Or that people *will* believe, in spite of all anathemas of creeds, that God will show a smiling face, instead of a vindictive one?

Rachel's mind was too much occupied by her absorbing passion to notice anything except the objects of her search. These she soon discovered, and in a place where she could fix her burning eyes.

The gilded balconies, and fluted columns; the graceful draperies of the proscenium and stage; the dazzling lights and crystal pendants; the sparkling jewels and expensive costumes, and even the favorite actors, in their mimic robes of royalty, were all blended in a kaleidoscopic view, with no distinct and separate forms. Two forms alone, in all that wilderness of beauty, were most fearfully distinct — John's — and Julia's.

Until the first act closed they did not notice Rachel. Then Julia took her opera-glass and looked around. As she took in the place where Rachel sat, she was at once arrested by Rachel's look. She was puzzled for an instant by something familiar in her face, and then, with some excitement, she turned to John, and handed him the glass, saying, as she did so:

"There is the very face that troubled me in my delusion! See! what a wicked look she has! And how she keeps her eyes upon us! Oh John! she makes me fairly shiver! Who ever heard before of an embodied phantasy? She has the very look of hate that I saw upon her face when she took you off!

"Nonsense! Julia. Don't get excited over an imaginary likeness to an imaginary form!"

But John, though speaking with a show of confidence, could not avoid a feeling of unrest.

"Which one?" he asked, as he raised the glass.

Julia described the place and person.

"Well! she *is* a starer!" muttered John.

"Did you ever see her anywhere before?" Julia asked.

"Never!" answered John.

"Well!" said Julia, "it is the strangest thing. See! She seems to look at you with fiendish hatred!"

"Let her look!" said John, bringing down the glass, and anxious to lead Julia's mind to other things.

But Julia could not resist a feeling of uneasiness, and as the second act commenced, and through all the play, she threw occasional glances across to Rachel. She always met the same immovable, vindictive look.

John turned in that direction, too, when he thought that Julia did not notice him; and with every look *his* uneasiness increased.

"They see me!" said Rachel to her companion; but she spoke without for an instant taking off her gaze. "See! how they look and talk, and talk and look! They see that they are detected, and will try to escape no doubt! But they'll *not* escape!" And like a vicious beast of prey she watched.

When the play was over, Rachel and the member started from their seats when they saw John and Julia start. Although their seats were on different sides, the distance to the door of exit was about the same. When John and Julia reached the door, and passed out into the lobby, Rachel and the member were immediately behind them. Before they reached the outer entrance, Rachel stepped up to John and wrathfully confronted him.

"How dare you flout me thus? and openly parade your shame!" she cried, in a loud, shrill voice. "Drop that huzzy; and come home with me!"

"Who are *you?* said John, in a sudden blaze of fury; but holding back hot words, in his anxiety to fathom this baffling perplexity.

"I am your WIFE! you wicked, perjured, and deceitful man! I'll not submit—"

Before she could finish what was already on her tongue, she, and all the crowd, were attracted by a sharp and sudden cry of anguish from the lips of Julia; and every eye was turned on her.

" See how she keeps her eyes upon us."

Her face was very white; and her eyes were wide, and staring, and fixed on Rachel.

"That is not a specter!" said she, speaking slowly. "I am not demented *now!* It is the face! the very face! and the very charge! the monstrous charge! O God! What is it all?"

John, now fearful of the worst results, took off the bridle from his tongue and let his fury fly.

With one arm supporting Julia, he pointed with his other hand to Rachel; and in a voice which broke like thunder on the air, cried out:

"ARREST THAT HAG!"

The words were like a killing blow to Rachel; and she staggered and retreated with a look of horror.

The member now rushed in—

"How dare you, sir!" said she to John.

"Another one?" cried John. "Are ALL the witches out to-night? Arrest *her* also!"

Julia now required all of his attention; for she seemed about to swoon.

"Make way there!" said he, as he almost carried her along to reach the open air.

John and Julia were accompanied by friends who knew them well, and who held them high in their esteem; and when they heard the monstrous charge, *their* indignation was not long unspoken. They turned on Rachel and the member, and demanded their arrest. An officer appeared and took them both. John, with some assistance, took the half-conscious Julia to the carriage, and sending a messenger for his physician, started for his house.

Rachel and the member, confounded by the situation, were taken to the station.

When Joseph went home to dinner, on this exciting day, Rachel was absent. This was not strange; for she was often absent now. He waited for her till long past the usual hour, and then took his dinner *solus*. After dinner she did not come; still he thought it nothing strange. Until nearly midnight, he expected, every instant, to hear her ring; but the stillness of the house remained unbroken. A chime clock on the mantel, with its silver tongue, rang out the *hour* of midnight; still Rachel had not come. He walked about the room; then sat down and tried to read; then he rose up and walked about the room again. So the dragging, anxious hours passed; and the chime began to sound like rhythmic voices speaking to his fears. He did not attempt to sleep, but walked and watched, until the sunlight of another morning slanted through the half-closed shutters of the room; still Rachel did not come. When the city was astir, and he could hear upon the streets the swelling hum of toil, he started out to look for Rachel.

Where should he go?

It was too early yet for the Ladies' Board. Perhaps he could gain some information through Mr. Pelter; and what Mr. Pelter knew his wife could draw from him. With this reflection he set out for Mr. Pelter's house.

Mrs. Pelter was much astonished by this early call, and very naturally supposed that it referred in some way to her husband.

"O, Mr. Smith!" said she at once, "why are you so hard on him? If you will only let him off, I will see that he does not trouble you again. If you are so angry that you will not favor *him*, then let him go on *my* account. You must know that he did not attempt to steal. It was his prying curiosity. He *is* sometimes almost a fool; but he is not a thief!"

"What are you talking of?" asked Joseph.

"Why, of my husband, to be sure."

"And what of him?"

"I want to get him out of jail."

"Out of jail! What's he *in* jail for?"

"Don't make light of it. You sent him there!"

"*I?*"

"You!"

"Why, woman, what's the matter with you? *I* never sent your husband or any other man to jail!"

Mrs. Pelter was so puzzled now that she knew not how to answer him.

She knew — as she supposed — that he *was* sent there by Joseph Smith; and what reason now had Mr. Smith for denying it? Perhaps, upon reflection, he had determined to ignore the whole affair, and thus avoid a public scandal. This seemed to her quite likely, and she resolved to trim to this new tack.

"Well," said she, with a knowing look, "suppose that it was *said* that he was held on your complaint?"

"I should deny it?"

"Would you? Truly?"

"Most certainly I should."

"And you will not testify against him?"

"No."

"Nor have your man?"

"Why no! Of course not!"

"Will you go with me and say you have no charge against him? — no criminal charge?"

"Most certainly I will; for in truth, I have no criminal charge against him."

"Well, you are a curious man. But you are very good to me; and you may have a hundred wives before I'll say a word against you; it's none of my business, anyhow! And Pelter would be better off if he had not made it his."

"*Now* what are you driving at?" asked Joseph, in a new bewilderment.

"No matter; mum's the word," said Mrs. Pelter, with a finger on her lips and a twinkle in her eyes.

"Let's talk of something, then," said Joseph, "that I can understand. Do you know where my wife is?"

"Which one?"

"*Which one!* Is *your* head filled with maggots too? Where is Rachel?"

"Why, sir, *I* don't know, I'm sure."

"I thought you might know through Mr. Pelter."

"Bless you! You forget that Pelter is in prison."

"Rachel may be in prison, too, for all I know," said Joseph, gloomily.

"That's not very likely," said Mrs. Pelter, with a smile.

"Anything is likely! Why, woman! if you should tell me to my face—and seriously—that I was not Joseph Smith at all, but William Jones, you would not surprise me in the least; and I would be more than half inclined to agree with you. I have been so badgered by perplexities that I am half distracted!" Saying this, he turned, and, muttering to himself, walked slowy off.

Mrs. Pelter looked after him, through a gathering mist about herself.

"He begins to muddle me," said she, as she went about her work.

Joseph could only wait until he could make inquiries of the ladies of the Board. He did wait. When he saw the Board, and learned where Rachel really was, his distress was touching.

Late as it was, on the night before, when Rachel and the Austere Member were taken to the station, a messenger was sent to arouse from sleep another member, and give the startling information that Joseph Smith had secured their arrest, and that they were now confined in prison. At an early hour in the morning a special meeting of the Board was called, to take some vigorous action as to this crowning outrage. They sent a member to the station, to interview the prisoners and learn the facts. When she returned and reported to the Board, their indignation was most furious.

"Whose turn next?" asked one, mounting the rostrum, and gesticulating wildly. "Is this man to take us, one by one, and plunge us into dark and loathsome dungeons? Where are all our boasted liberties?"

Another jumped upon a chair, and like a ranting sibyl on her tripod, called out excitedly:

"We have concealed his crimes too long! He has imprisoned those who saw his guilty acts, but *we* are free! and we know his crimes, and now we must proclaim them!"

These, and many other inflammatory speeches, wrought up their minds to a pitch of mad excitement, and in the very heat of it, Joseph Smith appeared.

"I come," said he, with his hat in hand, "to ask if you can give me any information as to my wife."

"Your wife!" repeated one, contemptuously.

"Yes; can you tell me where she is?"

"Hear the wretch! Pretending ignorance!" cried out the sibyl from her tripod.

"Wretch! Pretending ignorance!" repeated Joseph, in a daze. "I ask you where my wife is; if you know, please tell me; if you do *not* know, then tell me *that*, and I will retire."

"You know that she is in prison!" called out another member.

"In prison! My wife — in PRISON! For God's sake, madam, tell me what you mean. How can Rachel be in prison?"

"We know it all, sir; don't count upon our ignorance."

"If you know, then in the name of all that's merciful *tell* me."

"Who sent her there?"

"How can *I* tell?"

"O, you hypocrite! you sent her there!"

"*I* sent my wife — to prison! Why woman, you are MAD!"

"Perhaps you did not send our member there?"

"What?"

"Nor Mr. Pelter?"

"What?"

"This is not the first time that you have been before the Board pretending ignorance. But it will not save you. You have gone too far."

This Ossa on Pelion was too much for Joseph's shoulders, and he broke down.

"Ladies," said he, in a tired, sorrowful and even touching voice, "if you but knew the sad distraction in my brain, and could see how sorely I am badgered by perplexities, you would try to aid me, and *not* turn me off to wander, in my blindness, to paths more intricate. If you could but see my heart and feel its heaviness, you would pity rather than revile me; and if a spark of woman's tenderness yet lived among you, you could not offer me a stone when I cry for BREAD! You have no hearts! Good-day."

His manner was more impressive than his language, and when he slowly turned and went away, he left an awful hush behind.

Could it be possible that *they* were treading blindly in the mazes?

One said: "He had such a look of sincerity and sadness that I misdoubt."

Another said: "We have done him great injustice, if we *are* in error."

The monarch of the forest was once a tiny sprout. Convictions grow from questionings, and an innuendo, if artfully suggested, may swell to public rumor, and even change the face of empires before it dies. Joseph left a little seed of doubt when he went away, and even in that sterile soil a rootlet shot from it and commenced to GROW!

CHAPTER XI.

RACHEL ON THE STOOL OF PENITENCE.

Joseph wandered for a time like a somnambulist, repeating to himself, in an absent way:

"Sent — my wife — to PRISON!"

At length it flashed upon his mind that these charges must have some foundation, and that perhaps Rachel *was* in prison, and that he was falsely charged with sending her.

This thought aroused him in an instant. He made inquiries, and at last found one who knew of the arrest, and who informed him that the prisoners were perhaps already on their examination. Now he hurried on until he reached the court.

His wild, distracted look attracted all who saw him, and he forced a passage through the crowd to reach the front. When he reached the little open space before the justice, an officer in attendance said:

"Here he is."

All looked at him, and the justice asked:

"Is your name Smith?"

"It is," said Joseph.

"We are waiting for you," said the justice, "and the case has been already called."

Joseph did not seem to hear him, for he was looking wildly at his wife. Her eyes looked wicked, and were fixed on him.

"What have you to say as to the charge against these women?" asked the justice.

Joseph, with a sudden start, turned to the justice, and with a look of great amazement, asked: "What *is* the charge?"

"You ought to know," said the justice, in surprise, "since you ordered their arrest."

"I never ordered their arrest!"

"What? Here, officer! you made the arrest, I understand. How is this?"

"He did order the arrest, your honor."

"You're a——" Joseph commenced, turning on the officer.

"Stop!" cried the justice; "where was it, officer?"

"In the lobby of the theater, when this man — Smith — was coming out."

"I was never in a theater in my life," protested Joseph.

"Enough of that," said the justice, with impatience. "Tell me what you know of this affair."

"I know nothing of it!" answered Joseph.

"Nothing?"

"Nothing!"

"Swear him!" turning to the clerk; and the clerk swore Joseph.

"Now, sir!" said the justice, "tell me, on your oath, what you know of this affair."

"I know nothing! as I said before. I am in such a mist, and so amazed by what I hear that I begin to doubt the existence of what I see before me."

"Do you say — upon your oath — that you know nothing of it?"

"I do, sir."

"What do *you* know of it?" turning to the officer.

"I did not see the fracas," said the officer; "I was called in to make the arrest."

"Well!" said the justice, turning to the clerk, "if there is no evidence, let these women be discharged."

Then, turning to Joseph, with some severity he continued:

"You should not make complaints and authorize arrests, unless you intend to prosecute. It is trifling with officers and courts of justice."

"But," still persisted Joseph, "I never made complaint, and never authorized the arrests! There is some mistake——"

"I've heard enough! Stand back!" Then turning to the clerk he said: "Call the next case."

So, wondering and wandering more than ever, Joseph stood back.

Rachel and the Austere Member were at once discharged. As they passed out, they were obliged to pass the place where Joseph stood. Rachel would not see or notice him, although he tried in every way to attract her notice. The member drew up to the fullest height of her long, lean form, and turning up her nose, passed him with a sudden flirt—all the artificial flowers on her hat quivering sensibly, as though in sympathy with her indignation.

Joseph went out after them; but they did not stop or look around. He tried to overtake them, but they hurried on, and all at once they disappeared. He waited for their re-appearance, and walked back and forth, for so long a time that he at last concluded they had found another place of exit. Then he walked away.

As John left the theater, supporting the half-conscious Julia, and listened to the language of her violent hysteria, his mind was filled with curious questionings. What he had heretofore believed to be the creations of a distempered mind, now came in form and specific language. Here was Julia's white-faced woman, and the very charge. Here the woman claimed him as her husband. Here she tried to take him off with her. How had Julia seen all this in the pictures of her mind? Was there, in truth, some spiritual sense too subtle for our gross perceptions, which enabled some to read the future as an open page? He had heard men talk of such a thing, but he had regarded them as dreamers or as charlatans. Could it be possible that his wife had that intensely electrical temperament, or spiritual affinity, which enabled her to read from the book of mysteries? How, otherwise, *could* there be this correspondence of her previous fancies with existent facts?

These, and others like them, were but indistinct impressions flashing through his mind as they hurried home. The physician came soon after John arrived. He expressed the most confident belief that nothing serious would result. He gave Julia something quieting, and she soon dropped off in sleep.

But John was anxious, and did not retire; and he had no sleep that night. In the morning, when she awoke, he was at Julia's bedside to see if rest had strengthened her. Her eyes were bright and natural, and her mind was clear; but her brow and lips would occasionally contract, and discover her perplexity.

"Well, John," said she, "I am all at sea again."

"Do you doubt me, Julia?"

"No, John, I do not doubt you. If I had started on this ground of trust, I should not have wandered so. Was she arrested?"

"Who?" "The hag?"

"Yes."

"I'm sorry for it, for I believe *she's* crazy. Don't laugh, John; 't was you that made Pelter crazy, and *I* do not believe in it. He is simply foolish, and his head is filled with *her* insanity."

"I am sorry for her, too, if she is crazy."

"Why, she *looked* like it, and her frenzy was most unnatural. If it is ascertained that she is insane, that will account for many things; but there are *other* things which even *that* will not account for. When I attempt to solve the riddle I am involved in a score of mysteries, and here is where I am at sea. It's all a muddle, John; but I *do* believe in you in spite of all the mysteries; perhaps it is because she is such an ugly-looking woman, when I come to see her, that I do not think it possible for her story to be true. You have too much sense; yes, and too much honesty. But is it not strange that her face and charge so exactly fit the face and charge so prominent in my delirium?"

"That *is* strange — and I have thought of it

myself. Now, Julia, for awhile dismiss the mysteries, and when you are up again, and stronger, we will talk them over and try to sound them. I know why you trust me, and do not believe this woman's talk."

"Why, John?"

"Because you love me."

"Can't we love, and yet distrust?"

"Yes; but not for very long. Love is the cable; and distrust the hidden rock which chafes it. If the cable wears against the rock *too* long, it will surely snap."

If there was a shadow on her mind, it was banished by this blunt and impressive figure. With brighter eyes she answered:

"John, you are a splendid fellow! And I never loved you half enough! Let us keep *our* cable from the shoals, and above the fret of hidden rocks."

"*Amen!*" said John, with a trustful, thankful heart.

The morning hours flew. So absorbed was John in the sublimation of his love, that he did not think of Rachel.

When, in the afternoon, he thought of her, he suddenly exclaimed: "I must be off. My evidence will be required."

"Let them go, John!—let them go," said Julia.

"So I will, if they do not deserve a punishment; but I must go to secure their release."

"Go, then; and come back soon."

He did go. When he reached the place, the court was not in session — it had adjourned. He made inquiries as to the women whom he had caused to be arrested.

"What are their names?" was asked.

"I do not know," he answered.

"Describe them."

He described them.

"They have been discharged for want of evidence," was the business-like reply.

Not displeased at all on hearing this, John went home again.

When Rachel and the Austere Member so quickly passed from Joseph's sight, they were on a mission which, had they been less pious, would be called a vengeful one; they called it one of duty. It was to state their grievances, and to commence proceedings against Rachel's husband for the crime of bigamy. The case, as they stated it to the attorney, was so clear in every circumstantial detail, that there seemed to be no question as to Joseph's guilt. And when Rachel made the necessary affidavits, she did not dream that the concise and formal statement was, in all essential features, a pure fabrication, containing not a single tint of truth.

Until all this was done, and they had retired from the lawyer's office, and started home, Rachel's indignation and her anger held her up. Then reflection came; and she began to tremble in the presence of her work. The Austere Member, seeing her uneasiness, spoke to her. Darker—darker—darker! grew the oppressive phantoms of her mind, until she almost choked, and gasped for breath. Whiter—whiter—whiter! grew her face, until the muscles twitched and quivered with her great emotion. The woman's nature in her was struggling with her passions, and throttling them! At length she turned to the Austere Member, with such a look of piteous despair as would have most profoundly touched a heart of less austerity, and almost wailed:

"What have I done! O! what—HAVE I done!"

"You have done your duty!" said the member, without a touch of pity or a relenting look; and her jaws snapped shut, like a trap of steel.

There was no comfort there for Rachel, and she took away her eyes, and looked within herself; there was no comfort *there.* She lifted up her frightened thoughts to Him who says, "Vengeance is *Mine;*" and to the example of His suffering and uncomplaining Son; and there was no comfort THERE!

"He is guilty," said the member, "not only

of the charge, but of an outrage against our liberties!"

"O, unlucky day!" cried Rachel. "And *I* am his accuser!"

"Who but you *should* be his accuser?" asked the member.

Rachel, with a flash of passion, turned fiercely on her—

"You!" she cried, "and your associates! have goaded me to this! Where are your hearts? Where is all your boasted charity? Your hearts are stone! Your charity a lie! I've had enough, too *much*, of it."

Before the member could recover, Rachel started back. She hurried to the lawyer's office, and with breathless eagerness commenced: "Stop this thing! At once! I withdraw the charge! I *will* not prosecute my husband!"

Strong as she was; tearless as her eyes had been; she now broke down, and with tears, and moans, and self-accusings, she began to plead.

"My dear madam," said the lawyer, in surprise, "you should have thought of this before. The warrant is already out, and the sheriff is on the way to make the arrest. You are too late."

"Too—LATE!" cried Rachel, starting up. "I tell you that I withdraw the charge!"

"But you can not withdraw the charge. The charge once made is beyond your reach."

"But I am satisfied! I do not *wish* to prosecute!"

"You may be satisfied, and not wish to prosecute; and still you can not reach him now."

"Why?"

"Because he is accused of crime, and he must answer to the public; and it is a serious crime."

"I did not dream of this! O, sir! Send for a carriage! Quick!"

The lawyer hurried out to bring a carriage, and Rachel threw her arms upon the table and her head upon them, and gave way to lamentations. The lawyer soon returned, and helped her to the carriage.

"Where shall he drive?" the lawyer asked.

Rachel gave the street and number, then added: "Tell him to drive like fury! I will pay him well."

Then the door was closed, and the horses sprang from the cutting lash, and bounded wildly on. They reached the house in time to meet her husband. He was preparing to leave under the escort of the sheriff, who was waiting for him. When Rachel entered, Joseph looked up at her. A sudden flush overspread his face, then left it paler and more haggard than before. She stood a moment, uncertain what to do; and then, in wild abandonment, she threw herself upon him, and hung upon his neck — turning up her

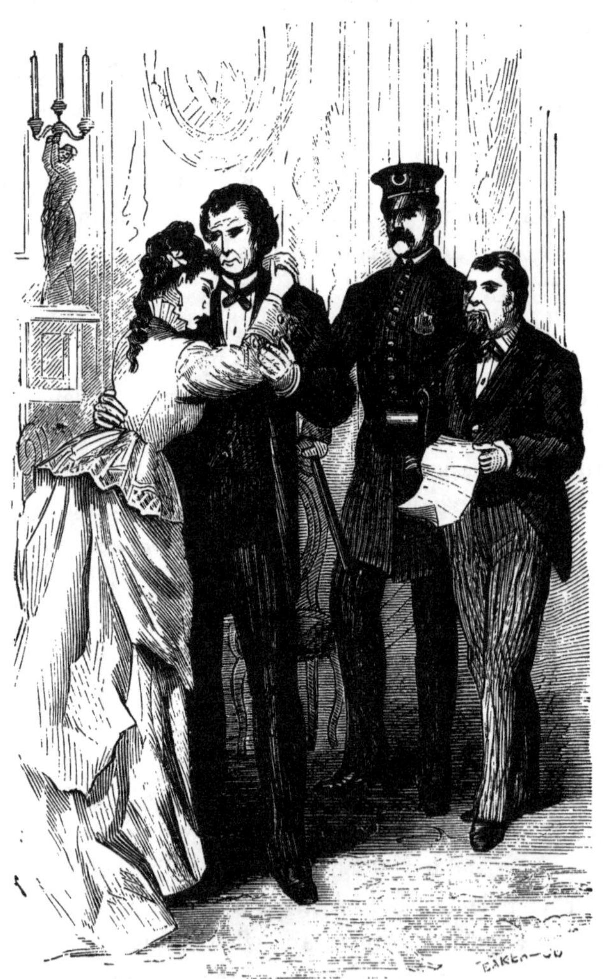

" She threw herself upon him, and hung upon his neck."

own white face to his, and pleading in a tone of agony.

"Can you forgive me? *Will* you forgive me? Speak! For mercy's sake! And tell me that you do not curse me for this most unwifely and unnatural act! Oh! To think that *my* hand strikes this cruel blow! And that my charge sends you to a prison-cell! But you shall not go! I'll swear that you are innocent, and that I was mad to call you guilty!"

"Calm yourself," said Joseph, gently taking off her arms. "I *must* go, Rachel. But you have lifted off a heavy burden from my heart. Have no fear as to the issue; for I assure you solemnly, and call God to witness, that I am innocent of every charge you ever brought against me. This must appear some day; and perhaps my trial may bring out the truth, and free me from perplexities."

"I beg your pardon," the sheriff interrupted, "but I have other matters requiring my attention, and if you can abridge this interview you will much oblige me. You may see each other as often as you please hereafter."

"*Must* you take him?" cried Rachel, with a beseeching look, which touched him sensibly.

"I must," he answered, "and do not — I pray you — make my duty harder by appeals to my compassion."

"The officer is right," said Joseph. "We should not keep him longer, and he shows his kindness and humanity. Do not accuse yourself too harshly, Rachel, for I know that I have been made to seem most guilty to you."

Then, turning to the sheriff, he said to him, "I am ready, sir."

Rachel did not follow them, nor cry out, nor speak a word. She *could* not follow them, or cry out, or speak. She was stunned and rooted to the spot. When the door closed after them she stretched out her arms, and groped for an instant, blindly, as though in search of some supporting object; then, with a moan most piteous to hear, she fell down, unconscious.

The servants had been watching, through an open door, in wondering amazement, and when they saw her fall, they rushed in and took her from the floor, and carried her gently to her room. They at once applied such restoratives as were at hand, and in a little time consciousness returned to her. She remembered everything. Then came long hours of meditation. When these were over, she arose, and there was an unfamiliar look upon her face; the rigid lines were softened, and there was no sternness in it.

"Thy rod!" and "Thy staff!" she would occasionally repeat, and the new dependence seemed to strengthen her. Self-righteousness was dead.

From that day Rachel was another and a nobler woman. Her conversations were no longer larded with sanctimonious formulas, but her daily life exemplified her faith, and made her grow in gentle charity.

CHAPTER XII.

MR. PELTER LEAVES THE MORAL HEIGHTS.

JOSEPH was taken to the city prison.

Mr. Pelter and some other prisoners, held for trial, were in the corridor.

Ezekiel was seated at the little table, beneath the grated window, engaged in writing. He was employed upon a new Pelterian tract, where, in exaggerated language he gave what he held to be a picture of himself, suffering for his righteousness. He was so absorbed in this employment, that the entrance of the sheriff with Joseph Smith did not disturb him. Even when the sheriff closed the door, with a loud and clanging sound, he did not look up. He did not look up till Joseph touched him on the shoulder and spoke to him.

When he did look up, and saw who touched him on the shoulder, he bounded from his chair, and with a frightened look, stammered out a broken exclamation of surprise.

"I told your wife," said Joseph, with a smile,

"that I would try and help you out of this. But now I am myself a prisoner, and my hands are tied."

"You! a — pris-on-er!" exclaimed the astonished Mr. Pelter, staring.

"Yes," said Joseph, "and yet, I'll help you, if I can."

"Bless me!" said Ezekiel, now recovered from his fear.

"Have you a lawyer to advise you?" Joseph asked.

"Yes," said Mr. Pelter, with his importance growing.

"When he comes," continued Joseph, "send him to me; I will give him information that may be of service to you."

"He'll be here to-day."

"Will your wife be here to-day?"

"She'll be here with the lawyer, sir."

"I must see her also. What does your lawyer say?"

"When I saw him first — at the station house — he said that I should sue you, sir, for damages."

"Indeed?"

"Yes sir; but I had damages enough."

"You thought it better to sue for some repairs, no doubt?"

"Well; yes; 't would be more reasonable."

"Then you really think that *I* caused your arrest?"

"THINK!" And here the good man fairly snorted.

"Yes."

"I know you did!"

And at the recollection, Mr. Pelter's warlike spirit began to stir, and frowns began to settle darkly on his brow. At this exciting juncture Mrs. Pelter and the lawyer were shown in. Mr. Pelter, with his majestic step, went forward to receive them. After mutual greetings, he pompously announced:

"The Devil's Emissary is at last in bonds!"

"That's good news!" said Mrs. Pelter. "And now I hope they'll catch his Imps — not neglecting those in petticoats; a few selections from your Board would be most wholesome."

Ezekiel groaned.

"But, to leave the Devil and his angels —" continued Mrs. Pelter, "I have good news for you."

"Ah!"

"Yes. There's something wrong about this matter of your arrest — I don't know what it is — but there's *something* out of gear. Mr. Joseph Smith declares that he has no charge against you, and that he will help you out of this. That's more than all your Board has done, or ever *will* do. They 're sharp enough to get you *into* mischief, but when you 're caught, they heave a pious sigh, and there 's the end of it."

"Why," said Mr. Pelter, "he 's the very man I spoke of!"

"When?"

"Just now."

"I did not hear you speak of him."

"He is the Devil's Emissary!"

"Pelter!—you 're a fool!"

At these familiar words, Ezekiel collapsed. With all his self-importance gone, he sighed, and meekly took his "cross." The quick, keen eye of Mrs. Pelter soon distinguished Joseph, and in a glow of honest sympathy she hurried up to him.

"Why sir!" said she, "what brings *you* here?"

"They *say*," said Joseph, with half a smile, and half a sneer, "that I have two wives. Some such notion seemed to be in your head when I saw you last, but then I did not understand you."

"Are you here for bigotry?" asked the astonished woman.

"Such a charge would be much nearer to the mark than bigamy," answered Joseph, smiling.

"Bigamy is what I mean, no doubt," said

Mrs. Pelter with a blush. "And that is why you 're here? Too many wives? 'T was hard to wait, I s'pose, for the ugly one to go to grass, and so you took the handsome one before the reg'lar time! Well, I 'm sorry for you — anyhow!"

"WOMAN!" said Joseph, in the voice so seldom heard, except when battling with the storms at sea. "I will not listen to such language!"

"Mercy! mercy! mercy! Do n't snap off my head!" said Mrs. Pelter, not at all alarmed. "What others make a monstrous crime of, and what, no doubt, *is* wicked and unlawful, I try to mention in a kindly way, because, somehow, my heart is with you; and for this you snap at me!"

"Oh woman! woman! will you never understand! All of this, every charge, and every innuendo, is a wicked lie! How these charges started, what they mean, and how it is that people seem to be so positive upon them, I have cudgeled my poor brains in vain to understand. If, as you say, your heart is with me, then let your lips take counsel from your heart, and not speak against me. Your husband seems to be somehow involved in these scandalous reports, and if your heart inclines you to my help, find out from him what it *is* I 'm charged with; not the *general* charge — that I have — but the *specific* charges. Let me get hold of something that

I can grasp, and hold, and throttle! and make an end of all this mischief! I cannot grasp these shadows! and if I attempt to stab them, I but. cut the air."

While he was speaking, Mrs. Pelter's faith in him increased till she believed him; and when he stopped, her heart was in her hand, as she held it out to him.

"No guilty man could look and speak like that!" said she. "He might deny, and swear, and all that, but 't would be in a different way. Now, with *all* my heart, I can work for you! I started in the wrong direction. I must go back and start again! This time I'll start upon your innocence. I'll hunt until I find some clue. I know *where* to look, for everything has come from one direction!"

Joseph, so all alone and friendless as he had been, and so frowned upon by saintly faces, felt this blunt and homely speech of friendship to the bottom of his heart; and as he took her hand, his lips began to quiver.

"Keep up your heart!" said she. "If I find the mischief where I expect to find it, I'll have some satisfaction on my own account."

"Where do you expect to find it?" inquired Joseph.

"In that Board of Gossips!" said Mrs. Pelter, spitefully.

"I wish that you could see my wife, and get her away from them; I know that they have filled *her* head."

"Ah! That's worth knowing! It gives a starting point! I'll see your wife; but perhaps she'll not *care* to see me. And I'll see that Pelter is no longer used to pull out chestnuts from the fire for them to munch, if he is a monkey! I'll keep him from that Board, if I have to tie him to my bed-post!"

Joseph saw that he had a sincere and earnest friend in Mrs. Pelter, and his heart took hope from what she said.

"Now," said he, "if you will send your hushand's lawyer to me, I will tell him — as I told you — that I have no charge against his client, and that I am ready at any time, and in any place, to say the same on oath, and that I know nothing of his arrest."

"Hear that," said Mrs. Pelter, with a show of some emotion. "You work to get him *out* of prison, and *he* works to get you *in! I'll* take a hand in this affair!" With this she turned and joined the lawyer and her husband.

"I wish that you would go and have a talk with Mr. Smith," said she to the attorney. "He will help us."

The lawyer went to Mr. Smith, and Mrs. Pelter turned upon her husband.

"Pelter!" said she, "you claim to be a Christian?"

"No one is perfect," answered Mr. Pelter, "and I am a child of sin; but so far as an angry God permits us to be good — I trust — I am."

"You *may be* a child of sin," said Mrs. Pelter; "and sometimes I think you are; but don't charge God with making you of any such material. Sin is the devil's clay, not God's. If it is in God's nature to hate *anything*, that is what He HATES! He don't make His children of such hateful stuff! If there is one thing above another that God *loves*, that one thing is goodness! And when you say that you are as good as an angry God *permits*, you say, in substance, that you would be a great deal *better*, if he did not keep you down. Now, Pelter, it is time for you to stop these slanders on the Almighty, and to understand that God tries, *always*, to lift us up, and *never* tries to keep us down."

"Oh, what blindness!" groaned Ezekiel.

"Do you suppose," continued Mrs. Pelter, "that God is pleased to see you and a lot of other meddlers always stirring up some dirty garbage, and spreading out your nostrils to take in offensive scents? Is He, in your opinion, so in love with things unclean that he likes to have

His children *smell* of them? Fudge! Pelter. It is too ridiculous."

"What are you driving at?" asked Mr. Pelter, more than half-ashamed.

"I want you to leave that crowd of scavengers!"

"What? The Board?"

"Yes; the B-o-a-r-d!"

"But how am I to live!"

"*Now — you've — spoken — it!*"

"What?"

"You hang upon their drabbled skirts, that they may *feed* you. Are you a dog?"

Her tongue was cutting like a lash, and Mr. Pelter winced at every stroke.

"Has Mr. Joseph Smith ever, in the world, done you an injury?" continued she.

"Yes!" he answered — glad that he had an answer.

"How?"

"Who sent me here?"

"He did not."

"He did."

"If he did he served you right; but he did *not* I say. There is some mistake in your arrest, and Mr. Smith is doing all he can to get you out. But *before* you were arrested; *then* had he ever injured you?"

"Why — no."

"And yet you spent days and nights in watching him. You fell into traps—bore the bites of dogs—stole into his house—poisoned his wife against him—all this you did to injure him who had never injured you. Is *this* the way that Christians work?"

"But he was wicked!" protested Mr. Pelter, trying, even yet, to hide behind his favorite cover, from his growing sense of meanness.

"When did God make YOU his flail? Oh, Pelter! Pelter! You have been wrong in this! Besides, he is not the wicked man you say he is."

"But I saw him!"

"I tell you there was nothing wrong."

"Sitting with a woman in his lap?"

Joseph's champion was hard pushed here, but she held her ground.

"You don't understand it! There was nothing wrong, I say! He is innocent of all the charges made against him, and it's coming out some day. He'll be right, and you'll be wrong! He has no other wife, that you have talked so much about."

She spoke with such assurance, that Ezekiel began to think that he *had* been wrong. Then he thought of all the mischief he had made, and all the unjust charges, and his heart began to sink.

"Why is he here?" he asked.

"You brought him here!" she answered.

"What — is — the — charge?"

"Bigamy! and it sends him to the penitentiary for a term of years if he should be convicted. This is *your* work! and the work of your Ladies' Board. This is your Christian work!"

Down stepped the paragon from his moral heights! Down dropped his head upon his breast! Down sank his heart, until it cried for mercy and forgiveness!

Mrs. Pelter was as quick to help as she was to punish, and when she saw Ezekiel down, she stretched forth her hand to lift him up again.

"Come! come!" said she, "do n't take my words too much to heart."

But he did take them to heart, and a new illumination filled his mind. Now he saw that all of his shortcomings, that he had scored against the Lord, were written on an open page, and charged against himself.

"I have often called myself a sinner," said Ezekiel, looking up, "but I never felt like one till now."

"And I 'll venture," said his wife, "that you never stood so fair as now in the sight of heaven."

Her speech was like a revelation to him, and he really felt himself to be a better man. Now, he saw in his long-neglected wife something to admire, and seeing it, and being "Pelter," he must speak his admiration.

"After all these years," said he, "I have just discovered that I left a jewel in my house, to amuse myself with artificial gems."

Who is too old or faded for Cupid's amorous pranks? Long athirst for some kind words from him, she drank these eagerly. And now the place where Mrs. Pelter's heart had been began to glow again, and the fluttering beats behind her corset gave notice that her love was tapping to get in once more.

With a smile and blush, which even gave a charm to her unhandsome face, she dropped her eyes and then looked up, and with a little laugh, replied: "La! Pelter! how you talk."

Ezekiel's flame was fed by this, and he stretched out his arms. But she eluded him, and with another laugh, and a glance at Joseph and the lawyer, said: "Not here — Pelter."

Joseph's case was brightening now, for even Cupid's bow was bent for him.

"What 's this?" said Mrs. Pelter, as she saw Ezekiel's manuscript upon the little table.

"It 's Pelter's last!" said he, and he took it from the table and destroyed it.

No more shall Mr. Pelter's stirring voice be heard in the ladies' rooms! No more shall Ezekiel's blandness beam upon the Board!

"I never was so puzzled in my life," said Mr. Pelter's lawyer, as he came back to them.

"How?" asked Mrs. Pelter.

"Why Mr. Smith declares that he did not know of the arrest of Mr. Pelter, and had no hand in it. He can't understand, he says, how it is that his name appears in it."

"Do you believe him?" asked Ezekiel.

"Yes, I do; that's why I am so puzzled. If I did *not* believe him I should not be puzzled. I can't help believing him; and yet I can not reconcile his statements with what you have said to me. Are you sure that he appeared to make complaint against you?"

"Well, no," said Mr. Pelter, "he did not *personally* appear; it was his man — his coachman."

"Ah! you did not tell me that. You always spoke of Joseph Smith."

"Because the coachman said that he was acting under orders."

"The coachman *said!* Why it may have been his own affair entirely. But how is it that the *name* of Mr. Smith appears upon the books?"

"Well," said Mr. Pelter, after a moment for reflection, "I did not think of it before, but *I* gave them his name."

"You!"

"Yes; they asked me who it was that ordered my arrest, and I told them Joseph Smith."

"Then, really," said the lawyer, with impatience, "everything he says is likely to be true; while you have been misled, and so have misled me — the blind leading the blind. No wonder that we stumble and fall into ditches."

"Things are coming 'round," said Mrs. Pelter, joyfully.

"I did not dream," said Mr. Pelter, "that I was misleading you."

"Well," said the lawyer, "we shall have no trouble in clearing you; Mr. Smith will secure that. But you will have to stay here for a few days yet, until the court convenes. I don't know but it serves you right for misleading me. If I had known the facts at first, you might have been discharged upon the examination."

"Perhaps I do deserve a little punishment," said Mr. Pelter, now as meek as Moses.

The lawyer left, and Mr. Pelter, turning to his wife, began: "Why, it looks as though I had been blundering in everything. I can't hold up my head before that man!"

"Nonsense!" said Mrs. Pelter; "the best of us may make mistakes; and many a man, and woman too, has done what, on reflection, would *never* have been done. This is what the preacher calls the weakness of our flesh. But, after all, it's only one among the marks we leave on *our* work to show that even patterns are defective.

Why, Pelter, men would all be gods if they had no blemishes; and they *would* be too — or the perfect copies — if they but kept themselves as God first made them. To confess a fault, and then to ask forgiveness for it, is a manly thing to do; but to deny it, or to try to crawl around it, is to play the coward — and cowards always hang their heads. Come now, let's go and talk with Mr. Smith."

With a braver front, but yet with hesitating steps, he followed her to where Joseph Smith was standing.

"This good man of mine," said Mrs. Pelter, "begins to think that he has injured you; and *like* a man, he wants to say so, and ask for your forgiveness."

This blunt speech was so different from Mr. Pelter's oily approaches, that it fairly frightened him, and he did not recover till Joseph offered him his hand. Then Joseph said to him:

"You have caused me trouble, but it is easy to forgive you, when you confess and honestly regret it. Now let's try to understand each other better."

Mr. Pelter took his hand, but he could not conceal a look of great astonishment.

"Why don't you speak?" said Mrs. Pelter to him.

"Oh!" replied the great exemplar, "I and

those with whom I have associated have been as blind as bats! *We* claimed to be the models of the world, and spent our time in thanking God that we were not like other men! No one among us ever thought of doing such a thing as you have done! When one injured *us*, or we *thought* he injured us, we followed him with maledictions! And when our lips repeated, 'Forgive us our trespasses, as we forgive those who trespass against us,' in our hearts we asked if the fires could not be made a little hotter for *our* enemies than for the *other* sinners."

"Now you're frank enough, at all events," said Joseph, with a smile.

"I have received instructions in a new theology," replied Ezekiel, looking at his wife, "and a better one, I trust."

"Talk your matters over now," said she, "and I will go and talk with Mrs. Smith."

"Thank you," said Joseph, with a look of gratitude. "I believe that all of us will profit by your 'new theology;' for I have heard your exposition."

With a look of satisfaction, the energetic woman left them.

CHAPTER XIII.

SOME VERY STRANGE DEVELOPMENTS.

RACHEL was much surprised when she saw the card of Mrs. Pelter; but she concluded to receive her, and so went in where Mrs. Pelter had been seated.

The meeting was embarrassing to both; but Mrs. Pelter, in her impetuous way, commenced: "I just left your husband."

"In prison?" Rachel asked, speaking with an effort.

"Yes," said Mrs. Pelter. "And *my* husband is in there with him."

"O! What an awful thing it is!" cried Rachel; and she hid her face behind her handkerchief.

"It's more likely to turn out in good," said Mrs. Pelter, "for now we begin to see the right of things."

"What do you mean by that?" asked Rachel, looking at her.

"Why, it seems that Mr. Smith had no hand

at all in Pelter's matter, and knew nothing of it; so you see that charge falls. Then, as to himself—your husband—and the charges made against him, it is likely to turn out that *they* were all mistakes. My lawyer thinks so, anyhow."

"Mistakes! Why, woman, Mr. Pelter saw him ——"

"There is the trouble!" interrupted Mrs. Pelter. "Pelter has a *won*-derful imagination!"

"Do you mean to say that your husband did not see him, as he said he did?"

"Well, he begins to thinks so now."

"Who begins to think so?"

"Pelter."

"He begins to think that he did not see what he *said* he saw?"

"Yes."

"Then how could he so mislead me? It was a wicked thing to do."

"As I said before, it was his imagination—his *won*-derful imagination! That Ladies' Board has practiced on it, and drawn him this way and that way by it, until they made him *think* he saw what he did not see at all. That Board was determined to make out a case against your husband, and they made use of Pelter and his wonderful imagination."

"Would you have me understand that the

Ladies' Board has been trying to make up a case?"

"Eggs-zact-ly!"

"What object could they have?"

"Why — as they say — it is their mission! They think, somehow, that they are the scourges of the Lord; and when no one *appears* for punishment, they *look up* some one to whip; they've made a fool of Pelter a hundred times, but now he's found them out and quit them."

Mrs. Pelter saw by Rachel's look that the Board was suffering at her hands, and she was sharp enough to let the impression work, without speaking more of it at present.

"Joseph certainly caused my arrest," said Rachel, with more confidence.

"No; you're mistaken there," said Mrs. Pelter, no less confident.

"I am not mistaken! Why do you think I am mistaken?"

"Because, at daylight, he came to our house to see if Mr. Pelter knew where you had gone."

"This morning?"

"This morning. He did not know that Mr. Pelter was in prison. When I told him of it he was much surprised. He was in distress because he did not know where you had gone. He looked as though he had not slept the night before. If he had you arrested, he would not come around in *that* way to look for you."

"Where was he the night before?"

"I do n't know that; but I thought from what he said that he was watching for you here all night."

"I will soon convince you," said Rachel, rising, "that you are wrong in that."

Here she rang a bell, and a servant came.

"Was Mr. Smith at home last night?" she asked.

"Yes ma'am," the servant answered.

"When did he come home?"

"He came to dinner, ma'am, at the usual hour."

"When did he go out again?"

"He did not go out; he waited here for you."

"How long did he wait for me?"

"All night, ma'am; he did n't go to bed."

"He went out in the evening?"

"No ma'am."

"But I saw him! I saw him at the theater!"

"If you say so, ma'am, of course I'll not dispute it."

"Then he *did* go out?"

"No ma'am—he did not. We all noticed it particular—and how he walked, and walked, and walked, all the evening, and all the night, and seemed so full of trouble."

"You may go," said Rachel, with such a baffled look as made Mrs. Pelter smile.

"I know," said Rachel to Mrs. Pelter, that Joseph was at the theater, for I saw him there; and yet the evidence is positive that he was *here!* What *is* the explanation? He told me, just before the sheriff took him off, that he was innocent of every charge—and he called God to witness."

"Do you wonder now that a man of Pelter's wit should make mistakes? Your husband and yourself are as much at sea as Pelter ever was. Did you ever think that this Board might be playing on *your* imagination?"

"No."

"Where have all these charges against your husband come from?"

"From Mr. Pelter and the Board."

"Pelter will retract! Does this not leave everything without foundation?"

"Except as to what *I* saw."

"Taking all you saw, can you say from that that your husband was really guilty of what was criminal or wicked?"

"Taking what I saw alone, it would not be sufficient. I took that with what was told me."

"And they took that in making what they told to you. Did you ever stop and ask yourself why they have taken up this thing so earnestly?"

"No."

"Can you understand it now, when I suggest it?"

"No."

"In· every new appearance, have they not always turned the worst side out for you?"

"I never thought of it before; but I think they have."

"Have they ever tried to put a *good* face on anything? even when there was a doubt as to appearances."

"I believe they never have!" said Rachel, growing more excited. "But I never looked at things in such a way before."

"Have they not made you absolutely see some things that you never could have seen without their spectacles?"

"It may be so—it *is* so! But why should they do it? I never injured them; and Joseph never injured them."

"They are MEDDLERS!"

And in that one word Mrs. Pelter's case was stated.

Rachel now began to look upon herself as much more guilty than before. Joseph's visit to the suspected house, from which she took him in a carriage, might have a proper explanation; and in fact he had attempted to explain, and she would not hear him. If Mr. Pelter should retract, where would be her charge of bigamy? She would not have a single fact to support the charge. Joseph's presence at the theater would not support it; and *that*, too, might be explained; besides, Joseph solemnly affirmed that he was not *at* the theater. How weak her case appeared in the light of Mrs. Pelter's strictures! How had it ever looked so strong to her? It must have been the magnifying glasses of the Ladies' Board! She had felt self-condemned for sending him to prison, when she believed him to be guilty; but now, that he might be innocent, her condemnation was increased a thousand times. Her very strength of character made her fault appear more monstrous than it would have seemed to many others, and it crushed her.

"Go back!" said she—in a sudden outburst of remorse, and kneeling on the floor before her visitor—"and tell my husband that you left me on my knees crying for FORGIVENESS!"

"No, no!" said Mrs. Pelter, lifting Rachel up. "I would rather take a different message to him—it would distress him less and help him more; besides, it is too late to go to-night."

"What message would you rather take to him?"

"I would rather tell him that, in your honest heart, you believe him to be innocent."

"Tell him that! I do! I do!"

"And that you will not associate with that Ladies' Board."

"Tell him *that!* God knows, I've had enough of them!"

"And that starting on an honest faith in him, you will join hands with me, and hunt these flying rumors until we catch and strangle them."

"Tell him THAT! I will! I will!"

"Oh why have I not talked with you before?"

"Because the 'Ladies' did not like me, I suppose; or my blunt ways of speech. I think that you had better see your husband; but not to-night, it is too late, and you need rest."

"I'll go to-morrow. And to-night I'll think of all you've said to me."

Mrs. Pelter left her thus, and as she trudged along toward home, she indulged in self-congratulations.

"A good day's work, I think!" said she. "Arranged for Pelter's freedom — pitched his idols over — emptied all his oil-cans — given Smith some comfort — and put his wife upon a smoother road to travel."

"This is an ugly business, after all," said a member, at a meeting of the Board, on the following day. "Did you say," (turning to the Austere Member) "that Mr. Pelter was in chains?"

"Yes; in heavy chains!" replied the Austere Member.

"They do not put chains upon a prisoner unless the case is a very strong and serious one," the questioner continued.

"I begin to think," remarked another, "that Mr. Pelter has not given us the truth in all these things."

"I think so, too," another said.

"How *can* you think so?" cried Miranda Trap.

"Because, the coachman swore ——"

"But," Miranda interrupted, "we have already said that the coachman was a perjurer!"

"I know we have, and I begin to think that we have said some *other* things that we should not have said."

"Why! What do you mean?"

"I mean," said the questioner, with spirit, "that we have been too quick in making charges!"

"Why! What has turned *your* head so suddenly?"

"Well, I began to feel uneasy about some things and I talked them over with my husband ——"

"With your husband!" cried several voices; and one continued, "Are we to take men's opinions in our affairs?"

"On such subjects," said the Doubting Member, standing stoutly up, in self-defense, "I think that men's opinions *are* better than our own."

This was heresy.

"Men's *opin*-ions!" said the Austere Member, with a snort, and turning up her nose.

"Well!" said the doubter, not to be put down, "*you* have been taking a man's opinion — and acting on it, too — and he not the most prudent man — in my opinion!"

"Name him!" said the Austere Member, with a frown.

"Mr. Pelter!"

"A-hem! But he is one of us," said the Austere Member, with some confusion.

"What did your husband say?" one asked.

"He said that Pelter was a blockhead, and that we should get rid of him; and that his piety was all a sham!" (Here Miranda flushed and looked quite furious.) "And he said that we had pushed on Mrs. Smith to make a charge of bigamy, when there was nothing to support it!"

"Humph!" said the Austere Member, throwing up her head.

"Why did not Mr. Pelter tell us," continued the Doubting Member, "*how* he entered what he called the 'abode of sin'? The coachman told before the court how that was! He was caught in a trap, and taken to the house, and there examined like a common thief! That is nothing *like* the story he made up for us to hear. And my husband says — and I agree with him — that we had better let such things alone; and instead of prying about our neighbors' houses, that we attend to missionary business — if we have any. Now, I have spoken!"

"I — should — think — you — had!" said the Austere Member, in a rage, for she was the nasal organ of the Board to collect domestic scents.

The courageous doubter found herself supported, and the party of reformers was soon respectable. They began to question *all* of Ezekiel's reports, and the husband of the doubter was thought by them to be quite sensible.

The discussion waxed furious at last, and the reformer's ranks grew stronger. Finally, the Austere Member stood almost alone, and no one would have dreamed, to hear her talk, that she ever could have been upon the moral heights.

Quivering with rage, and white with passion, she called to the gushing vessel, and these two together left the ladies' rooms, never to re-enter them.

So, having lost its nose, the Board cared no more for scents, and all their little microscopes were packed away. Then the members all looked up and saw their telescope, and going up to it, they cleaned off the rust and fixed the object-glass to take new images.

On that same day the Board received a strange communication, written in a cramped, irregular hand. They had never seen a specimen of Mrs. Pelter's writing, otherwise they might have known from whom it came. Without remark, or comment, or any signature, it read as follows:

"Thou shalt not go up and down, as a talebearer, among thy people." — (Lev. xix. 16.)

"The words of his mouth were smoother than butter, but war was in his heart; his words were softer than oil, yet they were drawn swords." — (Psa. lv. 21.)

"Whoso privily slandereth his neighbor, him will I cut off." — (Psa. ci. 5.)

"In the multitude of words there wanteth not sin; but he that refraineth his lips is wise." — (Prov. x. 19.)

"A froward man soweth strife, and a whisperer separateth chief friends." — (Prov. xvi. 28.)

"Where no wood is, there the fire goeth out; so, where there is no talebearer, the strife ceaseth." — (Prov. xxvi. 20.)

"Judge not, that ye be not judged." — (Matt. vii. 1.)

"For he that will love life, and see good days, let him refrain his tongue from evil, and his lips that they speak no guile." — (1 Peter iii. 10.)

The royal reveler was not more confounded by the writing on the wall than were the members of the Board by this strange communication.

"Who ever thought," said one, "that all of this was in that Book which we profess to take as our guide?"

"It condemns us all," another said. And all of them were visibly impressed by it.

That Board did not soon forget these words; and even *they* began to grow in charity.

Mrs. Pelter was at the city prison early in the morning. She reported her success with Rachel, and encouraged Joseph by her confidence.

Ezekiel had slipped and stumbled, through the night, as he tried to walk in her new way, and felt discouraged when she came. She brushed the oil from his shoes, and gave them a firmer hold when he stepped out, and he took heart again.

Rachel also came. It was observed by Joseph that she had never been so gentle as when she spoke to him of his confinement.

Now, for the first time since suspicion and distrust began to grow between them, they talked of all their troubles, and tried to understand each other. Everything was satisfactorily explained, except the story, to which Mr. Pelter still adhered, that he *did* see Julia in Joseph's lap, and the strange encounter at the theater. Joseph still insisted that he was in neither place; and he spoke with such sincerity that Rachel could not charge him with an intention to deceive.

"Perhaps," said he, "even this will be cleared up some day."

It was now plain to Rachel that her charge of bigamy could not be sustained; and in spite of the conviction that her own rage and jealousy were alone responsible for the present situation, she felt relieved.

After this, she would not leave her husband, except at night — when she was obliged to go — and then she would return on the following day. So, day after day, she came; and even in these prison walls they both became more free in all their thoughts than when surrounded by the walls of bigotry and self-righteousness, which closed them in from charity.

At length the day for Mr. Pelter's trial came. He was formally arraigned, and plead "Not guilty."

The room was full; for Mr. Pelter's "labors" had made him known to many, and they were curious to see if the great exemplar had been guilty of a crime. The coachman was present as a witness, but John was absent. Indeed, John had not been subpœnaed; for all the officers supposed that Joseph was the one who made complaint. John did not know, in fact, that the trial would be had that day.

Mr. Pelter, feeling certain of acquittal, was serene and bland. He bowed with dignity to the presiding judge, and to the sheriff, and to the prosecuting lawyer, and the curious audience; then he sat down, and spread his large and spotless handkerchief across his knee.

A jury was soon called, and properly examined,

and sworn in; and when they took their seats in the jury-box, Ezekiel bowed to *them*, and let his blandness shine.

"He's game!" said one in the crowded room, "and comes smiling to the scratch."

"Order in court!" the sheriff cried.

"Your honor," said the state's attorney, "the prosecuting witness — Mr. Smith — is now in jail, but he has not been tried, and is competent to testify."

The coachman, hearing this, pricked up his ears, and leaned forward.

"What is the charge against him?" asked the court.

"Bigamy," the attorney answered.

"What's that! what's that!" said the excited coachman, springing from his seat.

"Order!" cried the sheriff.

The coachman left his seat, and silently approached the sheriff, and in a whisper asked:

"Did that lawyer say that Mr. Smith was now in jail, and charged with bigamy?"

"Yes," said the sheriff, "you know it well enough. Sit down!"

The coachman stepped back to his seat again, but his face showed such perplexity that those around him were attracted by it.

"What's the matter?" asked one near him.

"That crazy Pelter *said* he had two wives!"

replied the coachman, "but who could ever have believed it?"

"Who had two wives?" the neighbor asked.

"Why Mr. Smith! my master! To think that he would serve my mistress so! She 's a angel, sir! And *he* was not a bad man. I 'll not believe it till I see him!"

"You 'll see him soon; they 'll bring him in."

While they were talking the court directed that Joseph Smith be brought, and the sheriff went out after him. The officer soon returned with Joseph Smith in charge.

"There he is!" said the coachman's neighbor. "Is that the man?"

Thomas looked at him, and instantly replied:

"Who ever *could* believe it?"

"Then he *is* the man?"

"Yes. Let me out of this! I must go and see my mistress! Poor thing! Poor thing! I must break it to her easy; for if she hears it sudden, 'twill be the death of her!"

Saying this, and in his great excitement not thinking that he would soon be called to testify, he rushed out, and hurried home.

The first witness called was Joseph Smith. He was sworn, and took the witness-stand.

State's Attorney.—"Will you tell the jury, Mr. Smith, what you know of this affair?"

Joseph.—"I know nothing of it, sir."

State's Atty.—"Nothing! Why sir, did you not order the prisoner's arrest?"

Joseph.—"No sir."

State's Atty.—"Was he not found prowling about your house?"

Joseph.—"Not to my knowledge."

State's Atty.—"Has he not been caught upon your grounds at night; and was he not caught near your stable, in a barrel?"

Joseph.—"Not that I am aware of. I never saw or heard of such a thing."

State's Atty.—"Well, this is about the coolest thing I ever saw! At the time of the prisoner's arrest, your honor, this man went to the station house, and there made statements which he now denies. The grand jury must investigate this thing!"

Joseph.—"I did not go to the station house, and I knew nothing of the prisoner's arrest until he was in the city prison. I do not believe that my coachman knows a thing about it—I never heard him speak of such a thing."

State's Atty.—"Why do you speak of your coachman? I have not mentioned him."

Joseph.—"I have heard the story, sir; and in the story my coachman is a character."

State's Atty.—"You are a cheeky fellow; but you shall answer for all this, my man!" (*Turning to the attorney for Mr. Pelter*) "Take the witness."

Pelter's Atty. — "I am satisfied."

State's Atty. — (*Furiously*) — "Call the coachman!"

The coachman was called, but he did not answer.

Sheriff. — "He was here when the case was called."

A Voice. — "He went home to break the news, he said, to Mrs. Smith; and to tell her that her husband was in prison."

Pelter's Atty. — "Mrs. Smith is here; and she knows her husband's situation; and has been in prison with him."

State's Atty.—"Another witness trying the game of dodge."

The Court (*to the sheriff*).— "Send for the coachman, and have him brought before the court!"

Mr. Pelter looked around the room with the greatest satisfaction. He seemed to say, in every look, "See! how innocent I am! and yet they have imprisoned me!"

He enjoyed the situation even better than he did his play when he clanked his chains in the city prison.

Mrs. Pelter, who sat by Rachel, back among the benches, quivered with excitement.

"Hear!" said she, as Joseph testified, "I told you that he knew nothing of it!"

"But what *is* the truth about it?" Rachel asked. "I am more confused by every fresh development."

"This proves more than that Pelter was arrested by some *other* person, and without the knowledge of your husband."

"What more?"

"Why, don't you see? If it was not your husband who saw Pelter in the barrel-trap — and Pelter told us both that he *was* caught there — then it was not your husband who was in the house! And *it was some other lap the woman sat in!* Whoever *that* man was, *he* came out, and saw Pelter in the trap!"

"Can that be possible? O! I hope so!"

"And if *that* is true, then, don't you see, if there *is* a man so much like your husband that Pelter could not see the difference, perhaps it was *that same man* that you saw at the theater; for, remember, he was with the very woman!"

"That would leave my husband clear of everything!" said Rachel, "and show that he had told the *truth* in everything. But how can one man be so like another?"

"There you have me," answered Mrs. Pelter.

"Joseph had a brother — a twin-brother —" said Rachel, musing, "who was so much like Joseph that he was mistaken for him often; but they have not met for over thirty years — and Joseph thinks that John is dead."

"Why have you not thought of this before?" asked Mrs. Pelter, much excited. "Why should your husband's brother be more likely to be dead than your husband? If your husband's brother *should* be here, we would have a key to all the mysteries. Then it would appear that your husband's brother was where he had a right to be, and where he should be — *with his wife!*"

"You reason like a lawyer," answered Rachel, admiring her. "With your clear brain, I could have solved the riddle, and saved myself from misery. I have been a blind and foolish woman, and I shall not blame Joseph if he never can forgive me."

"You go too far in saying that. He must admit that appearances convicted him, and that it would require a stronger faith than mortals have, to hold him guiltless in the face of them. As soon as we get out of this, we must search for this brother of your husband."

"What a comfort you are to me!" said Rachel, with emotion; "and yet the ladies told me that you were not a Christian."

"As they understand it, I am not," said Mrs. Pelter.

"But as you understand it?"

"I try to be," said the honest woman, with a look and tone of modesty.

"How *do* you understand it?"

"I can only state it in my simple way."

"And that is —?"

"To love God and trust in Him; and to believe that He loves me, and is not a monster to be feared."

There was a beauty in these simple words that Rachel had never found in all her austere creeds.

When Thomas, the coachman, reached John's house, he was so blown that he could scarcely speak. He sat down in the kitchen to recover breath.

"Why, Tom; what's the matter?" asked a servant.

Thomas only shook his head.

"What *is* it, Tom?" another asked.

"It's trouble! that's what 't is," said Thomas.

Now, more curious, the servants pressed him with their questions. But he only answered by an inquiry: "Is she home?"

"Who?"

"Mrs. Smith, of course!"

"Yes."

"Where is she?"

"Up stairs. But what *is* it, Tom?"

"Don't bother me! I want to think."

They could not get another word from him;

and he sat there silent, until he had determined on a way to "break it easy" to his mistress.

Then he left the kitchen and went up stairs. He met Julia in the hall, as she was coming from the family room.

She looked at him, then stopped and asked: "What is it, Thomas? You look frightened."

He looked down upon his hat, as he turned it in his hand, and answered slowly: "It's hard lines, mistress."

"What?" asked Julia.

"It's hard lines, I say; that about your husband."

"John?"

"Yes, ma'am."

"What about him, Thomas?"

"Why, ma'am—" and here he hesitated.

"Why don't you speak?" said Julia with impatience.

"It's hard to speak it, ma'am."

"What did you come here for? To try my patience? If you have anything to say, *say* it!"

"He's in trouble, ma'am."

"Who? My husband?"

"Yes, ma'am."

"I think not, Thomas. Why do you think he is in trouble?"

"Because—they've caught him."

"Caught him! How? What do you mean?"

"Why, ma'am, what that crazy Pelter said turns out true."

"What?"

"About the other wife; they've got him in the jail for it."

"Who have they in jail — Pelter?"

"Yes, he's there, too."

"He's there *too!* Why, do you think that my husband is in prison?"

"Yes, ma'am; I know he is."

Julia turned and opened the door just closed by her, and said: "John, come out here, will you? and see if you can understand this man."

John came out, and the coachman stared at him.

"What is it, Thomas?" John inquired.

"Why," said Thomas, staring still, "how did you get here before me?"

"Get here before you! Why, man, I have not been out to-day."

"The Evil One is in it, sir!"

"In what?"

"When I'm there, *you* are there; and when I'm *here*, you are HERE! *There* you are arrested, and in the sheriff's hands; *here* you are with your wife, and not at all arrested! It's too much for me!"

John and Julia looked at one another in amusement; and perhaps they wondered if the air was *not* infected; for the coachman's talk was more obscure than Pelter's.

"Come in here," said John, turning to the room again, "and I will see, if possible, what's in your head." They all went in.

"Now," said John, "where have you been?"

"To the court, sir."

"For what?"

"To give my evidence."

"In what?"

"In the trial of that crazy Pelter."

"Is he on trial?"

"Yes."

"*I* should be there, then."

"You *was* there!"

"What?"

"I seen you there!"

"You do not clear it much," said Julia turning, with a smile, to John.

"Hold on!" said John. "There's something in the fellow's mind, and I must try and follow it." (Turning to Thomas.) "What was I doing there?"

"The sheriff brought you in, sir, from the jail."

"Was I a prisoner, then?"

"Yes, sir."

"Ha! ha! ha!" laughed Julia. "How *very* clear you make it!"

"What was I in jail for?" continued John, motioning with his hand for Julia to keep quiet.

"For bigamy! So the sheriff and the lawyer said."

This answer struck both John and Julia instantly. Here was the same old charge. But now some other man was in John's skin to answer for it.

"Did you look at me?" continued John.

"Of course I did," said Thomas.

"But might you not have been mistaken? Might it not have been some *other* man you saw?"

"Will you turn and look into that glass?" said Thomas, pointing to a pier-glass.

John turned, and stood before the glass.

"Is *that* you? In *there?*" asked Thomas.

"No," answered John; "that is my image or reflection."

"Well," said the coachman, "when you can find among living men an image as *like* you as *that* is, then I'll say the prisoner might be that other man."

Such an image, among living men, flashed at once upon John's mind; and turning quickly to his wife, he said: "I wonder if it can be my brother Joe?"

"Was he like you?" Julia asked.

"Yes. But how can Joseph be in prison on

such a charge? He was a very pious soul; and, in fact, he was my pious father's pride, while I was the castaway and reprobate."

"His name *was* Smith," said Thomas, wondering. "That's what they called him."

"His name was Smith, and he is my image! It must be my brother Joe!" said John, with much excitement. "Julia, I must go and see what this trouble is, and help him out of it!"

"I hope," said Julia, "that he is not guilty of such a crime as Thomas says he's charged with. But I tell you, John, these sanctimonious men will bear close watching sometimes; they're no better than the rest of us; and too often not half so good."

"I'd like to see a better saint than you are," answered John. "But I must be off. Come, Thomas!"

When they arrived at court, Thomas was taken by an officer and brought before the court.

"Is that the witness?" asked the judge, with a frowning look on Thomas.

"Yes, sir," replied the officer.

"I am more than half inclined," said the judge to Thomas, "to send you to the lock-up!"

"For-wha-wha-what?" asked the trembling Thomas.

"For having left the court-room when you were wanted as a witness!"

Here John stepped forward.

"May it please the court," said he, "my man here," (indicating Thomas) "in his surprise and consternation, did not think of his surroundings, and ——"

"Why! what's this?" interrupted the astonished judge, as he looked from John to Joseph, and from Joseph back to John. "Another Proteus!"

This attracted all within the view, and others looked from John to Joseph, and from Joseph back to John. Now, there was a buzz, and whispers of astonishment.

"It is the KEY!" cried Mrs. Pelter, rising up in her excitement, and speaking in a voice which could be heard throughout the room.

"It is my brother JOHN!" cried Joseph, standing up, and looking at him.

"Yes, Joe! you 're right," said John, with a look and tone of gladness.

"Order in court!" the sheriff cried, and all was still again.

Now John continued — speaking to the court again:

"There is some strange mistake in this affair, I fear, resulting from the remarkable resemblance which you have observed between my brother and myself. If you will allow a little time for consultation, I have no doubt the ends of justice will be subserved by it."

"I never saw a resemblance so exact!" replied the judge. "Take time for consultation. I can now begin to see why your brother Joseph so persistently denied what we supposed to be the fact. Let the coachman take his seat."

Thomas took his seat. John went to Joseph, and they took each other's hands, and made such demonstrations of their pleasure as their situation would allow. Then they were joined by Mr. Pelter's lawyer.

Mr. Pelter was the picture of comic misery. The situation was so far beyond his misty powers of analysis, that he was incapable of coherent reasoning. As though he might find some inspiration there, he looked up to where his wife was standing.

She, with parted lips and sparkling eyes, grasped and fully understood the whole. By her side was Rachel, with hands clasped on her breast, looking pale and anxious, and her remorseful soul speaking in her staring eyes."

"O!" she hoarsely whispered to Mrs. Pelter, "why did I not trust my husband?"

Mr. Pelter's lawyer called the state's attorney to the consultation. Everything was now explained and understood between them.

"Then," said the state's attorney, "the case against Mr. Pelter falls."

"And so does the case against my brother Joseph, I should think," said John.

"Undoubtedly," replied the state's attorney. "No case can be made out against your brother, for he is innocent; his wife was entirely mistaken."

With these conclusions the conference closed; and the state's attorney addressed the court, explaining, in all their details, the curious, and comical, and serious mistakes which had ended in these prosecutions.

Joseph's innocence, as well as Mr. Pelter's, being thus made clear, both, by proper orders and proceedings, were at once discharged from custody.

"Come on!" was heard in a sharp and snapping female voice, from another portion of the room, and all looked to see from whom it came. A tall, lean form was seen making long and ungraceful strides for the outer door, and a shorter and meeker woman was following after her. Mrs. Pelter, from her position, saw them both, and she quickly recognized the Austere Member of the Board, and the now broken vessel, Miranda Trap. And so, without our benediction, they make their final exit from these veracious chronicles.

Mr. Pelter's eyes at last began to open.

"Bless me!" said he, "who ever *could* have thought it!"

John and Joseph, arm-in-arm, walked out, and waited near the door for Rachel and Mrs. Pelter.

"Oh Joe!" said John with a hearty laugh. "To think that I should have to get you out of such a scrape as this! Charged with bigamy! and going to a theater! Oh, Joe! Joe! Joe!" and he laughed again.

Here the impetuous Mrs. Pelter came through the door, and made a rush for Joseph, and caught him by both hands, and congratulated him.

"Evidently," said John aside, with his laughing eyes on Mrs. Pelter, "Joe is not fastidious as to *styles* in beauty."

"Where is Rachel?" Joseph asked, as soon as Mrs. Pelter gave him time to speak.

"She 's just inside the door," said Mrs. Pelter, "and won't come out until she knows that you forgive her."

"Don't she know me yet?" said Joseph. "I'll go *for* her, then."

He went, and came out again with Rachel on his arm. Her face was pale, and her eyes were filled with tears; but a light was shining through her tears, which made her almost seem attractive. Joseph led her up to John, and formally presented her. She blushed and stammered like a frightened girl; and John, to break the embarrassment, took her hand and said:

"I must first ask your pardon, sister, and then

I'll ask you and this wicked Joe to go home with me. Can you forgive me for my unbrotherly behavior in the lobby of the theater?"

Rachel blushed again; but now she looked at John, and admired his frank and smiling face.

"The fault was my own, I'm sure," said she, "and *I* ask *your* forgiveness, for insulting you and your charming wife."

"Charming!" answered John, with another laugh, "you did not think so then! ha! ha! ha!"

"This is Mrs. Pelter, John," interrupted Joseph, as he presented his courageous champion.

"Ah!" said John, with a twinkle in his eye, "I have entertained your husband I believe. I gave him the run of my gooseberry bushes, and let him play with Leo."

Now it was time for Mrs. Pelter's blushes; but for all of that she admired John.

"He made you trouble, sir, I know," said she.

"Oh, don't mention it," said John. "He took me once to his Ladies' Board, and there I met a gushing maiden ——"

"What's that?" cried Joseph.

"Why, Pelter took me to his 'Board,' and they wanted me to tell about the idol worshipers — it was rather in *your* line, that — and now, by Jove, though I never thought of it before, they must have thought that John — the bad boy — was the missionary, Joseph!"

"But who was the gushing maiden?" inquired Joseph, smiling at his brother's raillery.

"The 'maiden all forlorn'? They called her Trap — Miranda Trap. I met her after that one day upon the street, and she would n't look at me! And Pelter said — he was with her — that I had another *woo*-man!"

"Who was with you?" Joseph asked.

"Why, Julia — my wife."

"Do you know," said Joseph, "that those women have been swearing that *I* was the one who made that visit to the Board; and that I was walking with your wife that day?"

"Oh, Joe! you wicked fellow!" responded John, with a wink at Mrs. Pelter.

"Rachel!" said Joseph, suddenly, "where is Miranda's letter? That 's John's."

"Joseph!" cried Rachel, in real distress, "if you can forgive my folly, let 's go home."

John, seeing her distress, dropped his bantering tone, and said: "No! You must all go home with me. You'll find a sailor's welcome in his house and heart. And I want you to see my wife; for she *is* a charming woman!"

"Not to-day! not to-day!" said Rachel. "I *must* go home!"

"Give me your street and number, then," said John to Joseph, "and I will bring my wife around to your house."

Joseph gave the street and number, and with this they parted.

When John reached home he astonished Julia by an explanation of all the strange mistakes.

"Then," said Julia, "it was your brother's wife who watched us at the theater, and made that charge upon you in the lobby?"

"Yes," said John; "she thought 'twas Joe she saw with you."

"Well, I am sorry for her, for I know something of the stings of jealousy."

"I am sorry for her too, for she takes the blame of everything upon herself. We must go over there to-morrow, and you must try to comfort her."

"Yes. Then everything is clear, except my curious fancy as to Joseph's wife coming here for you, and your stealing off to her."

"And since that *is* a fancy, it can not be cleared," said John.

On the following day they drove to Joseph's house. Rachel was composed, and almost cheerful; and Julia's manner was so friendly and caressing, that Rachel was at once quite charmed.

When Julia was introduced to Joseph, he blushed, and was so sensibly confused that John remarked it.

"It 's all right now," said Rachel, as she saw Joseph's blush, and put her hand on Julia's shoulder; "but you must confess, when I did not know you, and saw you take Joseph in your carriage —"

"Take Joseph in my carriage!" repeated Julia.

"You took me home to lunch one day, you know," said Joseph, still uneasy.

"What!" cried Julia, "and asked you to take me to the theater?"

"Yes."

"Was that YOU?"

"Yes."

"I thought 't was John!"

Here Julia laughed, and laughed, and laughed, until the tears ran down her face; and then she held her sides, and cried, "O dear! O dear!" and laughed again.

"What is it, Julia? What is it, Joe?" inquired John. "If there's anything so funny let us all enjoy it."

"And I asked you to my *boudoir?*" continued Julia, ready to explode again. "You thought it rather free in a perfect stranger, I suppose. No wonder! Ha! ha! ha!"

Then Joseph told the story, and John began to laugh.

"What did you think, Joe? Did she scare you? 'T was well your name was Joseph!"

"I thought I'd better get away," said Joseph, "and—I did!"

"Did you pull your boots off?"

"Yes."

"And walk out slyly in your stocking feet?"

"Yes."

"And your wife was at the door to take you home?"

"Yes."

"And then you *caught* it?"

"Well — ra-ther!"

"Why, I made my wife believe—and I believed it, too—that that was all her fancy."

Then Joseph, the pride of Israel's heart, and John, the unregenerate, sat down to talk together.

Julia said to Rachel, as they sat down together: "All this would make a curious story, if written out and printed in a book."

And so thought the author of these Chronicles when he commenced to write.

GETTING ON IN THE WORLD; or, Hints on Success in Life.— By WM. MATHEWS, LL.D., Professor of English Literature, etc., in the University of Chicago. Beautifully printed and handsomely bound.

Price, 1 vol., 12mo., Cloth	$2 25	Half calf binding, gilt top	$3 50
The same, gilt edges	2 50	Full calf, gilt edges	5 00

CONTENTS: — *Success and Failure — Good and Bad Luck — Choice of a Profession — Physical Culture — Concentration — Self-Reliance — Originality in Aims and Methods — Attention to Details — Practical Talent — Decision — Manner — Business Habits — Self-Advertising — The Will and the Way — Reserved Power — Economy of Time — Money, its Use and Abuse — Mercantile Failures — Over-Work and Under-Rest — True and False Success.*

"A book in the highest degree attractive, * * and which will be sure to *pay in dollars and cents* many times over the cost of the work, and the time devoted to its perusal."—*Lockport Journal, New York.*

"It is sound, morally and mentally. It gives no one-sided view of life; it does not pander to the lower nature; but it is high-toned, correctly toned throughout. * * There is an earnestness and even eloquence in this volume which makes the author appear to speak to us from the living page. It reads like a speech. There is an electric fire about every sentence."—*Episcopal Register, Philadelphia.*

"There is no danger of speaking in too high terms of praise of this volume. As a work of art it is a gem. As a counselor it speaks the wisdom of the ages. As a teacher it illustrates the true philosophy of life by the experience of eminent men of every class and calling. It warns by the story of signal failures, and encourages by the record of triumphs that seemed impossible. It is a book of facts and not of theories. The men who have succeeded in life are laid under tribute, and made to divulge the secret of their success. They give vastly more than 'hints;' they make a revelation. They show that success lies not in luck, but in pluck. Instruction and inspiration are the chief features of the work which Prof. Mathews has done in this volume."—*Christian Era, Boston.*

THE GREAT CONVERSERS, and Other Essays.— By WM. MATHEWS, LL.D., author of "Getting On in the World."

1 volume, 12mo., 306 pages, with Map, price $1 75

"As fascinating as anything in fiction."—*Concord Monitor.*

"These pages are crammed with interesting facts about literary men and literary work."—*New York Evening Mail.*

"They are written in that charming and graceful style, which is so attractive in this author's writings, and the reader is continually reminded by their ease and grace of the elegant compositions of Goldsmith and Irving."—*Boston Transcript.*

"Twenty essays, all treating lively and agreeable themes, and in the easy, polished and sparkling style that has made the author famous as an essayist. * * The most striking characteristic of Prof. Mathews' writing is its wonderful wealth of illustration. * * One will make the acquaintance of more authors in the course of a single one of his essays than are probably to be met with in the same limited space anywhere else in the whole realm of our literature."—*The Chicago Tribune.*

THE WORLD ON WHEELS, and Other Sketches.—

By Benj. F. Taylor. Illustrated. 1 vol., 12mo. Price, $1.50.

"Full of humor and sharp as a Damascus blade."—*Presbyterian, Phil a.*

"The pen-pictures of B. F. Taylor are among the most brilliant and eccentric productions of the day. They are like the music of Gottschalk played by Gottschalk himself; or like sky-rockets that burst in the zenith, and fall in showers of fiery rain. They are word-wonders, reminding us of necromancy, with the dazzle and bewilderment of their rapid succession."—*Chicago Tribune.*

"Reader, do you want to laugh? Do you want to cry? Do you want to climb the Jacob's ladder of imagination, and dwell among the clouds of fancy for a little while at least? Do you? Then get B. F. Taylor's World on Wheels, read it, and experience sensations you never felt before! * * It is a book of 'word pictures,' a string of pearls, the very poesy of thought."—*The Christian, St. Louis.*

"Another of Benj. F. Taylor's wonderful word painting books. * * In purity of style and originality of conception, Taylor has no superiors in this country. The book before us is a gem in every way. It is quaint, poetical, melodious, unique, rare as rare flowers are rare. He has an exquisite faculty of illustration that is unsurpassed in the whole range of American literature."—*St. Louis Dispatch.*

OLD-TIME PICTURES and SHEAVES of RHYME.

By Benj. F. Taylor. Red line edition, small quarto, silk cloth, with eight fine full page illustrations.

Price...$2 00
The same, full gilt edges and gilt side........................ 2 50

John G. Whittier *writes*:—"It gives me pleasure to see the poems of B. F. Taylor issued by your house in a form worthy of their merit. Such pieces as the '*Old Village Choir*,' '*The Skylark*,' '*The Vane on the Spire*,' and '*June*,' deserve their good setting. * * I do not know of anyone who so well reproduces the home scenes of long ago. There is a quiet humor that pleases me."

"Unless it be Whittier, we know of no American poet so sweet, tender and gentle in his lyrics as B. F. Taylor. No writer of to-day sings the praises of rural life and scenery as eloquently, and we do not wonder that many of his poems have become classic. The holiday volume of his happy verses, Old Time Pictures and Sheaves of Rhyme is a very eloquent and daintily bound volume, and comes from that growing and reliable publishing house of the West, S. C. Griggs & Company, of Chicago. Taking up this handsomely printed book, we have to linger on the delightful imagery and graceful diction of its pages, glowing as they are with pure and tender thoughts, and the earnest, indescribable music of sunny fields and rural joys. * * No one can read it but will be the better for so doing."—*The Albany Morning Express.*

PRE-HISTORIC RACES OF THE UNITED STATES.

By J. W. FOSTER, LL.D., Author of "The Physical Geography of the Mississippi Valley," etc. 415 pages, crown 8vo, with a large number of illustrations.

Price, cloth	$3 50
Half calf binding, gilt top	6 00
Full calf, gilt edges	7 50

"One of the best and clearest accounts we have seen of those grand monuments of a forgotten race."—*London Saturday Review.*

"The reader will find it more fascinating than his last favorite novel."—*Eclectic Magazine, N. Y.*

"The book is literally crowded with astonishing and valuable facts."—*Boston Post.*

"It is an elegant volume and a valuable contribution to the subject. * * * Contains just the kind of information in clear, compressed and intelligible form, which is adapted to the mass of readers."—*Appleton's Popular Science Monthly.*

"The book is typographically perfect, and with its admirable illustrations and convenient index is really elegant and a sort of luxury to possess and read. * * Dr. Foster's style reminds us of Tyndall and Proctor, at their best. * * He goes over the ground, inch by inch, and accumulates information of surprising interest and importance, bearing on this subject, which he gives in his crowded but most instructive and entertaining chapters in a thoroughly scientific but equally popular way. We have marked whole pages of his book for quotation, and finally from sheer necessity have been compelled to put the whole volume in quotation marks, as one of the few books that are indispensable to the student, and scarcely less important for the intelligent reader to have at hand for reference."—*Golden Age, New York.*

A MANUAL OF GESTURE.—With over 100 Figures, embracing a complete system of Notation, with the Principles of Interpretation and Selections for Practice. By Prof. A. M. BACON.

Price	$1 75

"Prof. Bacon has given us a work that, in thoroughness and practical value, deserves to rank among the most remarkable books of the season. There has in fact, been no work on the subject yet offered to the public which approaches it for exhaustiveness and completeness of detail. * * It is of the utmost value, not merely to students, but to lawyers, clergymen, teachers, and public speakers, and its importance as an assistant in the formation of a correct and appropriate style of action can hardly be over-estimated."—*The Philadelphia Inquirer.*

"Prof. Bacon's Manual seems expressly arranged for the help of those who study alone and have undertaken self-instruction in the art of persuasive delivery. The work in the hands of our ministry, well studied, would have the effect of emphasizing the living words of the Gospel all over the land, and making them two-edged with meaning."—*The Chicago Pulpit.*

8

PHILOSOPHY OF THE PLAN OF SALVATION.—By REV. J. B. WALKER, D.D., with an Introductory Essay by CALVIN E. STOWE, D.D. A new edition, with supplementary chapter by the author. Sixty-seventh thousand. 1 vol. 12mo. Price, $1.50.

"Though written with great simplicity, it is evidently the production of a master mind. * * and few works are more adapted to bring skeptics of a certain class to a stand. * * It is the disclosure of the actual process of mind through which the author passes, from the dark regions of doubt and infidelity to the clear light and conviction of a sound and heartfelt belief of the truth as it is in Jesus.

"There is in many parts of this treatise, a force of argument and a power of conviction almost resistless.

"It is a work of extraordinary power. * * We think it is *more likely to lodge an impression in the human conscience, in favor of the divine authority of Christianity*, than any work of the modern press."—*London Evangelical Magazine, England.*

"No single volume we ever read has been so satisfactory a demonstration of the truth of religion, or has had so strong a controlling influence over our habits of thought. * * No better book can be put into the hands of the honest and intellectual skeptic. It is overwhelmingly convincing to reason, and leaves the doubter nothing but his passions and prejudices to bolster him up. * * Every minister's library should have a copy."—*The Methodist Protestant, Baltimore.*

"It fills a place in theological literature which no other book does. It is the style of the argument which gives power, impressiveness, and perennial freshness to this production. * * We have found in pastoral experience that we could place no better uninspired book than this in the hands of intelligent doubters, or in the hands of new converts, for their aid and guidance. Those who are not familiar with it, will do well to procure a copy and study it carefully. It is worth more than some large libraries to those who read for their profiting."—*The Christian at Work, New York.*

THE DOCTRINE OF THE HOLY SPIRIT; Or Philosophy of the Divine Operation in the Redemption of Man.—Being volume second of "The Philosophy of the Plan of Salvation." By REV. J. B. WALKER, D.D. Fourth edition, revised and enlarged. Price, $1.50.

"The author's former able works have prepared the public for the rich treasures of thought in this volume. It is a book of foundation principles, and deals in the verities of the gospel as with scientific facts. It is an unanswerable argument in behalf of Christ's life, mission, and doctrine, and especially rich in its teachings concerning the office and work of the Spirit. No volume has lately issued from the press which brings so many timely truths to the public attention. While it is metaphysical and thorough, it is also clever, forceful, winning for its grand truth's sake, and *every way readable.* The author has wrought a great work for the Christian Church, and *every minister and teacher should arm himself with strong weapons* by perusing the arguments of this book. It is printed and bound in the exquisite style of all publications which issue from Messrs. S. C. Griggs & Co.'s establishment."—*Methodist Recorder, Pittsburgh.*

www.ingramcontent.com/pod-product-compliance
Lightning Source LLC
LaVergne TN
LVHW020243110826
845151LV00003B/1020

* 9 7 8 1 4 2 5 5 2 8 9 7 3 *